WHERE IS HER CHILD?

Vicky gave a small sigh of pleasure—it was good to be outside in the garden after a week in the office. As she carefully patted the earth over a row of seeds, she thought of Ben and looked around. He must have gone around to the front.

"Ben!" she called. "Come on back here, honey."

She waited a moment and when there was no answer she marched around the side of the house and into the front yard. "I know you heard me," she began. Then her heart seemed to stop. The front gate swung open on its hinges, and Ben was nowhere in sight.

"Oh my God," she breathed.

BY
BEVERLY HASTINGS

A JOVE BOOK

DON'T TALK TO STRANGERS

Copyright © 1980 by Beverly Hastings

All rights reserved. No part of this publication may be reproduced or transmitted in any form or by any means, electronic or mechanical, including photocopy, recording, or any information storage and retrieval system, without permission in writing from the publisher.

Requests for permission to make copies of any part of the work should be mailed to: Permissions, Jove Publications, Inc., 200 Madison Avenue, New York, NY 10016

First Jove edition published May 1980

10 9 8 7 6 5 4 3 2 1

Printed in the United States of America

Jove books are published by Jove Publications, Inc., 200 Madison Avenue, New York, NY 10016

*To Big David, Little David
and Spike—with love*

Prologue

The seedy motel squatted under the crimson sky. Most of the bungalows were dark; their occupants had already gone in search of whatever nightlife the town could provide.

Bungalow number eight was ablaze with lights. The man in the bedroom stepped out of his Levi's and pulled his sweaty T-shirt off over his head. He moved casually to the window and snapped down the blinds, shutting himself off from the rest of the world.

In the bathroom the shower was running, forming clouds of steam that covered the mirror and began dripping down the walls. The naked man looked at himself in the dresser mirror. He liked what he saw. Young, vital, a healthy, virile animal. He tapped his fingers against his forehead in a salute to himself.

The sleek portable radio by the bed crooned melancholy songs on a local station. The man crossed to the nightstand and turned the volume up full force. Then he walked into the bathroom.

He looked with disdain at the paper bath mat supplied by the management. He reached out and yanked one of the thin bath towels down from its rack and threw it on the floor. There were still several hand towels as well as the larger one left. Surely even a dump like this would send someone with fresh ones tomorrow. He tested the water pouring down behind the plastic curtain, then he stepped into the tub. The water was already backed up ankle-deep. He picked up the minute bar of cheap soap and started lathering his arms.

A tall figure stood under the bathroom window of bungalow number eight. He listened to the sound coming from within, then he walked around the corner of the little stucco building. He tried the door; it was locked. Taking out a plastic credit card, he slid it between the door and the frame. The door opened easily. He stepped inside and closed it gently behind him. Then he stood still for a moment, listening.

The little radio blared out something about the Elks Club annual picnic, and went on with a string of other public service announcements. Over its noise he could hear the shower running and a voice singing off-key: "I can't get no sa-tis-fac-tion." He stepped quickly to the radio. Reaching down behind the nightstand, he jerked out the plug.

Still moving quickly, he walked into the bathroom, the radio in his hands. His rubber-soled shoes made no sound on the peeling linoleum floor. He balanced the radio on the edge of the tub and then shoved the plug into the outlet beside the sink. As the volume came up, he gently pushed the radio over the edge.

As it hit the water swirling in the bottom of the tub, the radio gave a series of quick, sharp, popping noises. The bungalow's lights dimmed momentarily and then came on again. The shower curtain bulged out and then sagged as the body behind it crumpled. With a dull thud like a melon splitting open, the head crashed against the faucet. The shower continued streaming, diluting the blood that oozed from the back of the skull and tinting the water in the tub pale pink.

The man turned away and walked into the bedroom. He picked up the wallet lying on the dresser. Ignoring the money, he pulled out the papers and looked through them systematically. Then he returned them to the pocket of the wallet and tossed it back on the dresser.

Moving to the door, he opened it, stepped outside, and closed it firmly behind him. Then he walked away toward the parking lot.

Chapter 1

"Ready for another glass of wine, Vicky?"

Vicky blew a puff of breath upward, dislodging a wisp of dark hair that was hanging over her eyes. Through the floor she could feel the pulsing vibrations of the disco dancers around her. She grinned at Larry.

"Thanks, but I think it's Cinderella time for me. I'd better get home."

Larry shrugged and said resignedly, "Okay, kiddo." Taking her hand, he forged a path through the onlookers crowded around the dance floor. He pushed open the exit doors and Vicky stepped outside gratefully.

"Whew!" she sighed, drawing a deep breath. "Thank God for some fresh air!"

"Really!" said Larry with a smile. "That place was turning into a mob scene." He put an arm around Vicky's shoulders. "Come on, The Pub is just down the street there. Guaranteed cool, dark, and quiet—just what the doctor ordered!"

Vicky shook her head and sidestepped out of his reach. "Sorry," she said softly, "I really do have to go home. My babysitter needs her sleep, and so do I. You know I'm a working girl."

"Aw, come on, we all have to work tomorrow. How about just a quick nightcap?"

"Some other time, Larry—please?"

Larry glanced once more at the beckoning lights of Westwood Village. "Sure you won't change your mind?" he asked.

"I'm sure," she replied lightly.

Larry dug in his pockets for the car keys as they turned toward the parking lot.

The dark blue Datsun sped westward along San Vicente Boulevard. Even this late in June, the Los Angeles night air was brisk and cool. As they crossed Lincoln, the fog rose up to meet them. At the end of San Vicente, they turned right onto Ocean.

"It's not far now," Vicky said. "Careful, it's a sharp right down the hill here. Just follow the road."

"I'm doing my best," Larry replied, peering through the windshield. "I can't see a goddam thing. How can you live down here in this pea soup?"

Vicky laughed easily. "I manage," she said. "Just take a left at this light, and Seaview is the first turn on the left."

He drew up in front of the small brown-shingled house. "Here we are, safe and sound." He reached across and pulled her to him.

Vicky's kiss was brief. "Thanks for a fun evening, Larry." Opening the car door, she smiled at him. "Do you know your way home now?"

"Oh, sure—left at the Coast Highway, and it's a straight shot down to the Marina. No problem."

"Good." Vicky slipped out of the car. "Thanks again, Larry."

As the Datsun's taillights disappeared around the corner, Vicky carefully latched the front gate behind her and started up the short walk to her house. The front door opened. A comfortable-looking woman, her short gray hair neatly framing her pleasant face, stood in the doorway.

"Hi, Mrs. Garfield. Everything okay?"

"Just fine," said the older woman. "Thought I heard you drive up. Have a good evening?"

Vicky grimaced slightly. "It was okay."

Mrs. Garfield picked up her teacup from beside the couch. "Nice to get out, though," she commented, clicking off the TV.

"I suppose. How was Ben?"

"Oh, we had a good time. He loves that new book you got him. And he stayed up till eight-thirty to see that 'Peanuts' show. Hope that was okay." She rinsed her cup at the kitchen sink and returned to gather up her knitting from the couch. "Hudson's really having trouble with that new little maid, Sarah."

This sudden jump didn't bother Vicky at all. She knew Mrs. Garfield's passion for "Upstairs, Downstairs." "I'm sure he'll manage. Any calls?"

"Just a wrong number, I guess it was. At least he didn't say anything."

"God, I hate those where they just hang on the phone, and then *click*. I've been getting a lot of them—it makes me feel all creepy." Vicky shuddered.

"Now, Mrs. Hunter. No need to worry 'bout the ones that don't say nothing." She pulled a police whistle out of her purse. "And this takes care of the ones with the filthy mouths. Just give 'im a blast of this in his ear and he won't try that again! You really should get a whistle and keep it by the phone."

Mrs. Garfield bustled toward the door, pulling on her sweater. "See you tomorrow."

"Sure you're okay walking home?" asked Vicky, though she knew what the answer would be.

"Sure as God made little green apples," said Mrs. Garfield with a laugh. And out she went.

Vicky turned and walked softly into her son's bedroom. She looked down at the sleeping boy. His arms were flung out and his coppery hair clung damply to his forehead. Gently, Vicky pulled up his blanket and smoothed the hair away from his face. "Tom's hair," she thought. "And my brown eyes." As she returned to the cozy living room, she reflected on how lucky it was that Ben hadn't inherited his father's pale skin. She remembered how easily Tom had burned in even the haziest sunlight, and yet how much he had loved living near the beach.

Vicky kicked off her shoes and sank down onto the couch. Mrs. Garfield was right, of course. It was good to get out. Like any other twenty-six-year-old woman, she enjoyed the attention men paid her. And she did like to go places and do things. It was a shame that she couldn't seem to get interested in anyone. Were they really all as boring as they seemed? she wondered. Or was she still holding Tom up as an ideal standard that no one could possibly meet?

"At least I have Ben," she said to herself. The thought of her bright, energetic, three-and-a-half-year-old son made her smile, even though his resemblance to his father was sometimes a painful reminder of all she had lost.

Vicky glanced at her watch and shook her head. Better stop feeling sorry for myself and get to bed.

"Hurry up, Ben. Don't dawdle over your cereal, honey," Vicky called from the bathroom. Of course, it had to be one of those mornings. The orange juice stubbornly remained a frozen lump—she should have moved it from the freezer to the fridge last night. One of Ben's sneakers had disappeared, only to be discovered behind his door after she'd pulled his bed away from the wall and managed to rip the seam of her shirt. Rushing to change into another outfit, she'd managed to knock her bag off the bed and then had had to spend more precious minutes crawling around the floor gathering up its contents.

"But I don't like Cheerios anymore. I already told you!" Ben called from the kitchen. Vicky checked her exasperation.

"Eat them anyway, hon. It's all we've got. Tomorrow we'll go to the store."

"But, Mom..." he started.

"Ben, the bus will be here any minute, and I want you to be ready." Thank God he likes his nursery school, she thought. I really couldn't handle an argument about that this morning, too.

The phone rang shrilly in the living room. Vicky heard the clatter of Ben's chair as he ran to answer it.

"Hello." There was a brief pause. "Ben," he responded into the phone.

"Who is it?" Vicky raced out of the bathroom to find her son holding out the phone to her with a puzzled look.

"I dunno," he said as she grabbed the receiver out of his hand.

"Hello? Hello?" There was no sound at the other

end, but the silence was alive. "Hello?" Vicky tried again. Then the connection was broken with a definite click.

"Oh, damn!" Vicky muttered as she slammed the receiver on its cradle.

Just then, the tinny horn of the minibus sounded outside. Vicky yanked open the door and helped her son into his sweatshirt.

"Have fun at school today, sweetheart. Mrs. Garfield will be here when you get home." She kissed him, and then walked with him to the front gate. Its latch was purposely too difficult for three-and-a-half-year-old fingers to operate.

Ben climbed into the minibus and turned to shout, "Bye, Mom!"

Vicky waved in reply, then closed the gate and hurried back inside. A few minutes later, she was backing her faithful VW beetle down the driveway.

Waiting for the light at the left turn onto San Vicente, Vicky flipped the radio on.

"... so for you folks heading north on the Harbor Freeway, it looks like they'll have that number-two lane clear any moment. Now, it's eight-twenty-seven and time for the weather," chirped the familiar voice. "How's it look for today, Joe?"

The light changed at last and Vicky swung the little car onto the boulevard. Eight-twenty-seven already—she certainly wasn't going to be early for work today. Still, traffic on San Vicente was moving right along, and if she didn't get hung up crossing on Bundy to Olympic, she'd be in pretty good shape. As the radio burbled on in the background, she wondered why, no matter when she turned on the news, she always heard the traffic report for the other side of town. People in

Pasadena probably only got to hear about problems on the San Diego-Santa Monica interchange.

At five minutes to nine, Vicky turned up the off-ramp for the Avenue of the Stars, and automatically made the quick right and left turns that took her behind the Century Plaza Hotel and into the back parking lot of the studio. It was enough of a hassle getting to Fox every day; thank God she didn't work out at The Burbank Studios. She'd really hate being stalled on the freeway twice a day.

Walking quickly across the parking lot toward the studio buildings, Vicky reflected ruefully that she was lucky to have this job at all. When Tom had died two years ago, she hadn't really known where to turn. It was bad enough to be a new widow with a one-and-a-half-year-old toddler. And since she'd married Tom right out of college, she had no work experience. True, Vicky had enrolled in graduate school and started working for her master's degree in her favorite field, Middle English, but she'd dropped out when Ben was born. It took her no time at all to discover how unqualified she was for any kind of position. Just as she was running to the end of her resources, a friend of Tom's had heard of an upcoming vacancy in the story department of 20th Century-Fox. Vicky had jumped at the opportunity and, with the friend's help, landed a job as an assistant story editor. It didn't pay very well, but the work was interesting and it was fun to be part of the moviemaking industry.

Vicky reached her office just as Sam from the mailroom came by with his cart. As he dumped an armload of large envelopes on her desk, Vicky exclaimed in mock dismay, "Oh, Sam, those aren't all for me?"

He laughed. "They keepin' you busy enough?"

"And how! Be sure to stop by on your way back. I've got a load of stuff to get out in the early delivery. Don't just think this is a one-way street here!"

Sam groaned loudly and moved on down the corridor.

"Hey, Vicky honey!" Cindy's familiar Southern twang floated across the hall. "Y'all want some coffee? I just put up a fresh pot."

"Sure," Vicky called back. "Thanks!"

She sat down and began opening the envelopes stacked in front of her, sorting their contents into three different piles. Cindy appeared in the doorway with two steaming mugs.

"This one's yours," she said, setting one cup on Vicky's blotter and pushing a heap of scripts to one side so she could perch on the corner of the desk. "Sure wish I liked this stuff without sugar and cream, the way you do." She tugged her skirt down over her plump knees. "On Monday I'm gonna start that Lake Forest diet."

Vicky sipped her coffee. "Oh, is that a new one?" she asked. "What happened to the Scandinavian one you were on?"

"Oh, honey!" Cindy exclaimed. "All that pickled herring, and nothing for breakfast but Ry-Krisp! I was starving to death!" She leaned over, watching as Vicky pulled a sheaf of papers out of an envelope. "Dear Lord! Don't tell me you sent that 'Peephole' script out for readers' reports! I read it last week and I declare, Vicky, I was blushing on every page. That trash is not fit to be read!"

Vicky smiled at Cindy's vehemence. "But I bet you read the whole thing, didn't you?" she teased.

"Well, of course! I had to find out how it ended,

didn't I?" Cindy laughed and went on, "Listen, honey, let's have lunch in the commissary today instead of going off the lot."

"Fine with me. It'll be cheaper anyway."

Cindy nodded. "Ain't it the truth! I just don't know where my money goes. But let's go early—you know Robert Redford is shooting on the lot today. He's such a gorgeous hunk, that boy!"

Vicky laughed again. "Trust you to know everybody's schedule! Now, get out of here and let me get some work done, or I'll have to skip lunch altogether. I've got a meeting with Ruth-Ann this afternoon."

"Why, sure, honey. See y'all later."

As Cindy drifted out, Vicky picked up a pencil and attacked the first pile of papers on the desk.

"Well," said Cindy as she wiped the chocolate from her lip with her napkin, "isn't he the most gorgeous thing you ever saw?"

Vicky murmured her agreement while chewing on her apple.

"I declare, if *he'd* been my midnight prowler, he'd never have gotten away!"

"Midnight prowler!" Vicky exclaimed. "What are you talking about?"

Cindy casually spooned more sugar into her coffee and giggled. "As it turned out, it was nothing. But last week I heard this *shuffle, shuffle* in that alleyway behind my bedroom. It was late and dark and I was plenty scared! And I didn't know what the goodness to do. I mean, should I call the cops or what? No way was I gonna look out the window and see who it was. He coulda had a gun or something! I mean, if some boy wants to take a peek, that's one thing, but what if he was dangerous or something?"

"What did you do?" asked Vicky.

"Well, I just stayed hid under the covers for a while. My heart was thumping so hard I thought you could hear it a block away. But I figured whoever he was, he'd hear me if I went to the phone. Besides, I can't see a thing without my contacts. How could I call the cops without putting on the light?" Cindy paused. "So I just waited, hoping he'd go away."

"Did he?"

"Not exactly. There was all this rustling around. Then there was quiet. Then I thought I heard the old gentleman who lives upstairs with his wife. He was climbing up the stairway in the front. I thought, if only I can slip out to the front door and call to him, he can do something. So I crept out of bed—you know I only had on this real pale blue nightie, and my robe was in the wash—and I got to the front door and opened it quiet as a mouse. 'Mr. Jeffreys,' I called, real quiet-like. And the man on the stairs stopped. 'Oh my gosh, Cindy!' says this man, and it *was* Mr. Jeffreys. 'Mr. J., I'm so glad you're here,' I told him. 'There's someone prowling around out back!' And then I really was embarrassed, because it was poor old Mr. J. himself out there. He'd thrown away the instruction book to his new video game by mistake, and he was worried the trashmen would come by early and it'd be gone. He said he was trying so hard not to disturb me. And I declare, Vicky, I was so relieved, I felt like giving that old man a big kiss!"

Vicky put down her coffee cup and stared at Cindy. "Wow, that must have been really scary. It gives me the shivers just hearing about it. I mean, this time it turned out to be nothing, but who can tell? There are a lot of weird folks out there."

Cindy nodded vigorously. "Ain't it the truth! And for a single girl living alone, it's hard to protect yourself—well, *you* know what I mean, Vicky. Don't you ever get scared all by yourself in that little house of yours? You don't even have any upstairs neighbors."

"Yes, I do," Vicky said slowly. "And it's not just prowlers. I've been getting these phone calls. You know the kind—when you answer the phone, no one says anything, and then, after a few moments, they just hang up."

"Oh, *those* creeps!" Cindy said disgustedly.

"Yes, well, the thing is, I can't tell if it means anything. It could just be a wrong number and they're not polite enough to say so."

"Or it could just be the dumb phone company screwing up as usual," Cindy broke in.

"And the problem is that there's nothing you can do about it. But it really is spooky."

"I know," said Cindy. "But at least you can always hang up."

"I guess you're right," Vicky said uncertainly. "But I still don't like it."

Vicky sat at the kitchen table, watching her son spoon baked beans into his mouth. She smiled at his determination and obvious enjoyment. Wouldn't life be grand, she thought, if all your hopes could be fulfilled with a dinner of hot dogs and baked beans?

"Mommy," Ben said between spoonfuls, "Mrs. Garfield is mean. I don't like her anymore."

"Finish what's in your mouth before you talk, honey," Vicky reminded him gently. "Why don't you like Mrs. Garfield?"

"We went to the park this afternoon, and she wouldn't let me stand up on the swing!"

"Honey, it's pretty dangerous to stand on the swings. I think Mrs. Garfield didn't want you to get hurt."

"But all the big kids stand up when they swing!"

"Well, when you're big, you can too. How was school today?"

"I'm mad at Michael. I was drawing a pretty picture for you, Mom, and Michael took my red crayon. He broke it."

Vicky smiled at her son. "I'm sure your picture is lovely, honey. Besides, Michael probably didn't break the crayon on purpose."

"Yes, he did!"

"What did you do then?"

"I told him that when my Daddy comes back, he'll come and beat Michael up!"

Vicky's eyes saddened. "Ben, we've talked about that—you know Daddy's not coming back."

Ben stopped for a moment, and then went on, changing the subject. "There was a man outside the gate today."

Vicky's pulse quickened. "Who was he?" she asked, trying to keep her voice calm.

"I dunno. Mrs. Garfield talked to him." Ben finished the last bite of his hot dog. He looked up at his mother. "I wish Daddy would come back."

Vicky reached across the table and stroked her son's arm, both to get his attention and to reassure him of her presence. "I wish so, too, sweetheart. But Daddy can't come back, Ben. You know that, don't you?"

Without another word, Ben got up and left the table. Vicky's eyes filled with tears as she cleared away the dishes. Carefully, she stacked them in the dishwasher. I really don't know what to say to him about his dad, she thought. He can't possibly remember Tom; he was only a year and a half old when Tom died. Would it have been better if I hadn't talked to Ben so much about his father? she wondered. But she'd wanted so badly for him to realize he had had a father who had loved him. She was sure it was important for Ben to connect up with the part of his family he'd never truly known. Ben loved to look at the picture of Tom in its silver frame on her dresser. Now she wondered if she had made a mistake.

It all seemed so unfair. That horrible accident in Arizona had snuffed out Tom's life just as his career was blossoming. They'd had less than three years together—a perfect, truly wonderful marriage.

—Well, not really perfect.

Quickly, Vicky thrust the disloyal thought back to the dark recesses of her mind. I must just concentrate on the good memories, she thought. That's what's important for Ben.

Vicky turned on the dishwasher and walked into the living room. There was Ben on the floor, surrounded by his blocks, busily engaged in building a fortress. He was so totally engrossed in his project that the reassuring phrases she'd decided on remained unsaid. She gazed down at her son. In his concentration, he was so like Tom. A fierce rush of protectiveness engulfed her.

He's all I have, she thought. God, don't ever let anything bad happen to *him*.

Then Ben grinned up at her. "Lookit my neat fort, Mom. Can't I leave it for tomorrow?"

"Sure, sweetie," she replied.

His delighted "Oh boy!" filled her heart; it took so little to make him happy. She watched him as he carefully added towers to each corner of the block fortress, secure in the knowledge that his creation would still be standing when he woke up the next morning. I'm all he has, too, she realized with a pang.

The late-morning sun warmed the soil of the back garden. Vicky sat back on her heels and surveyed her small house with satisfaction. It was a simple two-bedroom cottage, built in the pre-Depression heyday of summer hideaways at the beach. The brown-shingled walls showed signs of age, but the mass of ancient bougainvillea spreading a crimson carpet over the garage at the side gave it a charm no architect could reproduce. The house sat on an odd-shaped lot whose corner was cut off by the flood-drainage canal. A high wall bordering the canal not only prevented access to its dangerous banks, but also provided support for trellises of green beans, sweet peas, and climbing roses in Vicky's garden. The remainder of the property was enclosed with a sturdy picket fence, whose two gates led to the front sidewalk and the driveway at the side.

The yard in front was a minute plot of grass with a border of colorful marigolds and pansies against the house. The triangular patch between the garage and the north side of the house was in constant shadow. Overhung with the bougainvillea, it was a jumble of old camellias and leggy shade azaleas. But the backyard was Vicky's pride and joy. Many hours of patient labor had transformed an unattractive, weedy plot into a flourishing garden of flowers and vegetables. A grassy area for Ben's tricycle marathons, and a small sandbox in the corner, kept him busy and content while Vicky coaxed her plants into bloom.

She leaned over to inspect the row of artichoke plants. They looked healthy; the damp beach air must agree with them. Maybe next year there would be artichokes for dinner. Vicky gave a small sigh of pleasure. It was good to be outside after a week in the office. I can make this garden exactly the way I want it, she thought. It's mine... well, mine and the bank's.

Vicky opened the packages of lettuce and Swiss chard seeds, and began to sprinkle them gently into the shallow furrows she had dug. As she carefully patted the earth over the rows of seeds, she wondered if there was room for a pumpkin patch. Ben would love to watch his own jack-o'-lantern growing in the backyard.

Thinking of Ben, she looked around. He must have gone around to the front; she didn't see his trike out here, either.

"Ben!" she called. "Come on back here, honey."

She waited a moment, and when there was no answer, she called again. "Ben? What are you doing?"

He was awfully quiet, and like any mother, she considered that ominous. What was he up to now? She hoped he wasn't beheading all the marigolds, or digging for worms between the pansies. She started around the side of the house. "Ben! I'm talking to you!"

Vicky marched into the front yard. "I know you heard me," she began. Then her heart seemed to stop. The front gate swung open on its hinges, and Ben was nowhere in sight.

"Oh my God," she breathed.

In a flash she was out on the sidewalk, looking anxiously in both directions.

—That damn mailman must have left the gate open. I'll kill him!

"Ben! Ben!" she shouted. "Where are you?"

At that moment the mailman came around the corner. With dismay she realized that he couldn't have left the gate open; he hadn't even gotten to her house yet.

Vicky raced along the sidewalk toward the mailman.

"Have you seen my little boy?" she asked breathlessly. "You know—red hair, brown eyes. The gate's open and he's gone!"

"Gee, no. Sorry, Mrs. Hunter," he answered slowly. "And I didn't see him anywhere on Entrada—I just came up there. How long has he been gone?"

"I don't know!" Vicky turned and ran frantically the other way, toward West Channel, the busy street that emptied directly into the Pacific Coast Highway.

At the corner, she stood for a moment, her heart pounding rapidly. "Ben! Ben, where *are* you?"

She looked up the street toward the mountains and the little park. If he'd gone that way, at least the traffic wasn't so bad. But she saw no sign of a small red-haired boy on a green tricycle.

Turning toward the ocean, she called again for her son. He wasn't on the sidewalk—she had a clear view all the way to the highway. Suddenly, from behind a parked car, a small figure appeared in the distance. Short legs pumping furiously, Ben was running headlong down the street, chasing his runaway trike. He was only a few yards from the weekend traffic racing up the coast.

Vicky's breath caught in her throat. Before her brain could transmit the message, her feet were already flying down the pavement.

"Ben! Ben, stop!" she screamed. "Come back!" But she knew he didn't hear her; the roar of the traffic drowned her cries.

The tricycle rolled relentlessly along the roadway, just clearing the parked cars and picking up speed as it went. Ben tried vainly to catch up with it. Each time he reached out to grab it, the trike leaped forward out of his grasp. It almost seemed eager to lead them both to destruction.

Vicky's bare feet were almost noiseless on the concrete sidewalk.

"Help!" she screamed, hoping some passerby would see what was happening. "Please, someone help!"

Where was everyone? The sidewalk ahead of her was deserted. Had everyone already gone down to the beach on this sunny Saturday morning?

As Vicky crossed the last sidestreet before the highway, she momentarily lost sight of Ben. The row of parked cars on West Channel hid his small form. In a panic, she veered out into the road, heedless of the sharp bits of gravel cutting into her feet. There he was, only a few car lengths ahead! With a surge of energy born of desperation, she plunged after him.

Still careening madly, the tricycle's left rear wheel hit a loose stone. Bouncing into the air, the three-wheeler sheared sharply to the left and crashed into a parked car. As it jolted to a stop, Ben lunged forward and grabbed the seat with both hands.

Vicky ran the last few yards separating her from her son. He was within arms' reach. Suddenly, out of the corner of her eye, Vicky saw a car coming straight toward them from the highway. It was moving fast, and the driver obviously hadn't seen them. Vicky snatched up her son. Whirling, she flung him onto the hood of the parked car and threw herself across him, shielding him with her body.

The driver of the oncoming car swerved violently into the middle of the street. His tires screeched as he slammed on his brakes and looked back to make sure the woman and child were unharmed. "Idiot! Keep your kid out of the street!"

As he gunned his motor and shot away, Vicky stood up, clutching Ben to her breast. Still holding him tightly, she pulled the tricycle onto the sidewalk, then sank to her knees. The reaction had set in. She was shaking violently all over, and tears were coursing down her face. Gathering her son to her, she rocked back and forth, murmuring over and over against his cheek, "Oh, Ben."

At last, Vicky rocked back on her heels and pushed him away gently so that she could look into his face.

"Ben, listen to me. You must never, ever go out into the street by yourself. You could easily have been run over by a car. Do you understand?"

Ben looked at her solemnly. "Yes, Mommy." He reached out and touched her wet cheek. "Don't cry, Mommy."

She hugged him tightly. "Oh, sweetheart, I was so scared." Leaning back and smoothing the hair away from his forehead, she went on, "What were you doing in the street, anyway? We've talked about that so many times."

"I know, Mom, but I got off my trike to pet the kitty and then my trike went in the street and I couldn't catch it."

Vicky shook her head. "You must not go in the

street by yourself for any reason at all. No matter what." She took a deep breath. "If your trike or any other toy goes in the street, you come and find me. I'll go and get it back. Okay?"

Ben nodded. Vicky stood up and brushed herself off. Her pulse had steadied, and her breathing was back to normal.

"Let's go home now," she said.

Vicky clasped her son's hand in one of hers, and grabbed the handlebars of the tricycle with the other. Together, they slowly walked back toward home. She felt completely drained, but the whole terrifying episode wouldn't stop replaying itself in her mind. She kept returning to the image of the front gate hanging open.

"Ben," she said, "how did you get out of the front yard? I didn't think you could open the gate."

"I can't," he replied. "A man opened it."

Puzzled, Vicky asked, "What man?"

"I dunno," he said. "Just a man."

"Was he looking for me? Did he say anything?"

"He said what's your name and I told him and then he opened the gate. I thought he was coming in, but then he walked away."

Vicky stopped and looked down at him. "Ben, was this man real or pretend?"

"He was real, Mommy. He just opened the gate and went away."

A wave of uneasiness sent a shiver down Vicky's back. She looked around. The familiar street suddenly seemed strange, even unfriendly. Then she shook off her irrational fear. As they walked up the front steps, she said cheerfully, "It must be time for lunch. What do you want to eat?"

Chapter 2

Vicky tasted the spaghetti sauce that was bubbling quietly in the big pot on the back burner. As she gave it a stir, she looked out the window at the overcast sky. Sure doesn't look like this will burn off, she thought. It may be a little chilly at the beach this afternoon.

She poured herself a fresh cup of coffee and carried it into the living room. Ben looked up from his coloring.

"Look, Mom, I made a picture of a tree," he said. "Now I'm going to make the sun on top."

"Good, that'll be nice," Vicky replied absently as she sank down on the couch and curled up with the "Home" section of the Sunday paper. The rest lay scattered on the floor.

Three minutes later, the phone rang. As Vicky padded across to answer it, she thought, I hope someone is there this time when I pick it up. Then she gave herself a mental shake.

—Don't be silly, no one's out to bother you.

"Hello?"

The deep male voice at the other end sounded friendly. "Hi. Is Tom there?"

Vicky stood clutching the phone, unable to speak. Her mind whirled. No one had said that for more than two years. The caller's words brought back that time when her grief and pain were almost too raw to bear. Memories of that whole period in her life flooded over her.

"Hello? Hello? Is this Tom Hunter's house?"

Vicky's attention snapped back to the present. "Yes," she said shakily. "Who is this?"

"You must be Vicky," said the man on the other end. He was beginning to sound embarrassed. "My name's Matt London. Tom and I went to college together. Have I called at a bad time?"

"No," Vicky said slowly. She took a deep breath. "Tom mentioned you often, used to talk about you a lot."

"Used to?" Matt tried a little laugh that didn't quite come off.

"Tom died two years ago."

"Died! Oh my God! What happened?"

"It was an accident." She paused. "He was on location, shooting a picture in Arizona, and he was electrocuted."

"Oh my God!" Matt said again. "I'm really terribly sorry. You must have had quite a time of it." Vicky murmured in agreement. "Just you and the boy alone now?" Matt went on. "How old is he?"

"Three and a half."

"And does he look like Tom? Same red hair and all?"

Vicky laughed. "Yup. Same red hair."

There was a pause. "Well," Matt said finally, "I hardly know what to say. This is really a shock."

"Yes, I know," Vicky said. "Where are you calling from?"

"As a matter of fact, I'm in Malibu." He went on to explain, "I've got a van and I'm driving down the coast. When I realized I'd practically pass right by your front door, I thought I'd call and see if we could get together. I was hoping to get to meet you at last, and of course to see Tom's son, and ... well, I guess I've been out of touch a long time."

"Well," Vicky said slowly.

Matt hurried to fill in the silence. "What's your son's name again?"

"Ben."

"Oh, right—and he's three and a half already? Wow, it's hard to believe." He went on more hesitantly, "I sure would love to drop by and say hello, just for a few minutes. If you wouldn't mind," he added.

By now, Vicky had recovered from the shock of Matt's first words. "Of course I don't mind," she said warmly. "The only problem is, we're going out in a few minutes and we won't be back until four o'clock."

"Oh, that's okay. Four is fine with me. You're at 19 Seaview Avenue, right?"

"Yes. See you later, then."

"I'm looking forward to it." His voice dropped slightly. "And Vicky, I'm really sorry to hear about Tom."

"Thanks," she said quietly. "Goodbye."

Vicky hung up the phone. But before she had time to

sort out her feelings, the doorbell rang. Ben rushed to open it. "Jimmy's here, Mom!"

On the doorstep stood a bright-eyed boy about Ben's age, with his father.

"Here he is," the man said to Vicky.

The two boys rushed immediately into the living room, and Vicky said, "Gosh, George, you look exhausted. Want to come in for a cup of coffee?"

"Oh, no, thanks anyway. I've got to get down to the hospital for fathers' visiting hours," he replied with a smile.

"Oh, I know. How's Sue?"

"Well, she's fine, but she's awfully tired. She had kind of a rough time," George said.

"Yes, I haven't called her yet because I thought she'd probably rather sleep," Vicky responded. She went on eagerly, "Tell me about the baby."

"She's gorgeous, of course," George said with a laugh.

"Of course!" Vicky laughed too. "Have you decided on a name?"

"We're still torn between Diana Lee and Jennifer Elise." Shaking his head ruefully, he went on, "We didn't have any trouble choosing a boy's name, but this is the first girl in my family for two generations, and everybody's trying to get in on the act!"

Vicky laughed again. "Well, I'm dying to see her, whatever her name is! Be sure to give Sue my love, and tell her to let me know if there's anything I can do."

"You're doing plenty as it is," replied George. "I sure appreciate your taking Jimmy this afternoon."

"It's no problem—we'll take the Frisbee down to the beach and have a good time."

"Well, thanks again," he said. "I'll come by for him

around four. 'Bye, Jimmy," he called. "See you later."

As he got into his car, Vicky turned to the children and said, "Well, boys, are you ready to go to the beach?"

The cool, overcast weather had kept everyone but a few hardy joggers away from the shore. Vicky loved the beach when it was like this—it had an air of mystery and intriguing possibilities that she never felt on bright, hot days when the sand was littered with half-nude, baking bodies. She could almost believe she'd turn to see Grendel emerging from his cave, or a sea serpent rising from the slow, gray waves.

She watched the boys sail the Frisbee back and forth, scrambling across the sand. Jimmy seemed to share his father's excitement about the new baby sister. Thinking back to Ben's first few days, she smiled wryly. She'd hardly known how to change a diaper. But she had loved learning to take care of her baby. The whole process had been fabulous. From the beginning of her pregnancy, she'd felt healthy and glowing, and the delivery had been much easier than she'd expected. It had been one of the happiest times of her life.

Of course, Tom hadn't felt quite the same way. He'd been anxious to have a child, but as her slim body thickened, he'd become remote and distant. Her changing shape seemed to turn him off.

Maybe all men felt that way—she didn't know. She supposed she couldn't blame him for finding pleasure elsewhere; he was an attractive, virile man. All along, he'd assured her that it was purely a physical need and that he cared only for her. But she'd been angry and hurt, and things had never again been the same between them.

We could have worked it out, she thought. I could have learned to satisfy him if only we'd had more time together.

The fog never did burn off completely, and by late afternoon, the air felt dank and cold. Matt's blue van coasted to a stop in front of Vicky's little house. As he climbed out, the front door opened. There stood a slender, dark-haired young woman with enormous brown eyes. She looked young and vulnerable—too young to be a widow. As he closed the gate behind him, he called, "You must be Vicky."

"Yes," she replied, holding out her hand. "And you must be Matt."

The room's warmth was welcome after the dampness outside. Matt glanced around in appreciation. Someone had lavished time and care on the inexpensive furnishings, creating a comfortable, friendly atmosphere.

"And here's Ben," Vicky said, indicating her son, who was lining up some cars on the floor. "Ben, this is Matt London. He's an old friend of Daddy's."

"Hi, Ben," said Matt in a hearty voice.

Ben gave him a long, appraising stare. "Hello," he said. Then he turned to Vicky. "Mom, can I make the cars have a big race?"

"Sure, just don't be too noisy," she answered. Waving Matt toward the couch, she asked, "Would you like something to drink? Coffee? Or some wine?"

Matt smiled at her. "A glass of wine would be great." Folding his tall frame onto the couch, he leaned forward. "Looks like you really like cars, Ben."

"Yes," Ben answered without looking up.

Matt went on, "I'll bet you've never seen one like

mine. I have a van that's like a little house. It has a bed and a place to cook and a little tiny TV."

"Can I see the TV?" Ben asked.

"Sure. The van is right outside."

"Mom! We're going to see a TV in a car!"

They all trooped outside, and Matt opened the van's side door with a flourish. "All the comforts of home," he said, grinning.

Vicky and Ben stepped inside. Every available inch had been cleverly used to provide maximum storage and living space.

On the far side, a handsome, natural-wood cabinet covered the wall from floor to ceiling.

"Go ahead, open it," Matt urged.

Vicky gasped in delight as the open doors revealed a complete miniature pantry and food-preparation area. Drawers, slots, and sliding trays kept everything neatly organized and accessible.

"This is fantastic, Matt! Who built it?"

"I did," he replied with a modest grin.

"Wow," she said respectfully.

Ben climbed up onto the platform that stretched across the rear of the van. Pointing to the shelf high up on the side wall, he said, "There's the teeny tiny TV."

"Right you are," said Matt, turning it on. "That platform's my bed, lounge, chair—a real all-purpose item," he explained to Vicky with a laugh.

Vicky silently took in the faded but beautiful Oriental rug covering the platform, and the storage drawers for clothes and bedding underneath. Mounted on the wall opposite the TV were bookcases, their metal-grilled doors holding a tightly packed collection of books and papers firmly in place. A hinged table hung flat against the wall beside the raised platform.

Everything in the van was ingeniously fastened in place. Behind the passenger seat, just next to the side door, there was even a high, small rack from which hung a plastic clothing bag, nestled against the wall.

Following Vicky's glance, Matt said, "That's for my dress-up duds."

Vicky turned around wonderingly. "It's incredible, like a ship, everything all battened down and tidy. From the outside, no one would ever guess. You're a real man of mystery."

Matt laughed.

From the house came the sound of the ringing phone. Vicky hopped out of the van and ran to answer it. Over her shoulder, she called back to Matt, "Don't let Ben keep you out in the cold forever. Your wine's on the coffee table."

Matt turned to Ben, who was already engrossed in the TV. "Well, what do you think?"

"Neat. Can we go for a ride?"

"Not right now," Matt replied easily. "But one day I'll surprise you. I'll come and get you, and we'll just drive away."

"Okay," said Ben. The two of them started back to the house.

Vicky finished her call as they came in. "I've just been getting to know your son," Matt told her.

"Good." Vicky sat down and kicked off her shoes. "Well, tell me what you're doing down here, Matt. I thought you lived up in Portland."

"I do," he said. "Or at least I did. I just got fed up with the ad-agency business and decided to strike out on my own. I know it sounds crazy, but I've always thought I could be a pretty decent writer, and I decided now was the time to find out. So I'm giving myself six months to see what I can do."

"Wow," Vicky said, sipping her wine, "that takes guts."

"Well, I figure I can always find another agency to hire me. I'm good at turning out ad copy; I just don't like doing it anymore."

"Sounds like you certainly cut yourself loose," Vicky commented. "But," she said hesitantly, "I thought Tom told me you were married."

"Yeah, well, I was, but we split up a couple of years ago. It turned out we wanted different things out of life. She's back in New York, working for a fancy investment firm." He laughed shortly. "But what about you? What do you do with yourself? Are you working?"

Vicky didn't usually talk much about herself, but Matt's obvious interest overcame her reticence. His gentle questioning drew her out, and before long she had told him all about her work, and the struggle she'd had finding a job when Tom died.

"It's a long drive every day," she wound up, "but it's a lot better than being on welfare!"

Matt looked at her in surprise. "But didn't Tom's—"

"You mean the insurance?" Vicky finished for him. "There wasn't very much, and I'm trying hard to save it for Ben. It'll pay for part of a college education, at least."

She saw Matt give her a speculative look. "That's all there was?" he asked. "Just the insurance?"

Vicky shrugged. "Tom wasn't earning all that much. Being an assistant movie producer is more glamour than income. And of course, I was in school and then home with Ben. We hadn't started thinking about saving yet."

"Couldn't your family help you?"

"Oh, my dad died when I was a kid. Mom finally passed away just a year before Tom died—she'd been ill for a long time. After the hospital bills, there was hardly anything left."

Matt shook his head. "You've really had a rough time. But how about Tom's family?"

Vicky looked mildly astonished. "Tom's parents were killed in a plane crash almost ten years ago. He didn't have any family. You must have known that."

"Of course. I don't know what I was thinking of."

"Vroom, vroom!" Crawling under the coffee table, Ben pushed his red racer toward the couch. It met Matt's foot with a thump. "My car crashed, Mom," he cried in delight.

"So I see," said Vicky. "Better take it back to the garage. Ben, five more minutes and then it will be bath time—I think you brought half the beach home with you."

Matt said quickly, "But I thought I'd take you both out for dinner."

"Matt, that's nice of you, but tonight would be just too complicated. Besides, I've already got something on the stove."

"Oh." He sounded disappointed.

"But you're welcome to stay and eat here, if you'd like. It's only spaghetti, but there's plenty of it."

Matt accepted with alacrity. Vicky refilled the wineglasses, then left Matt watching the news on TV while she put Ben into the bathtub and got dinner under way. Dumping the boxful of dry spaghetti in the pot of boiling water on the stove, Vicky set the timer.

"Hey, did you hear that?" Matt called over the murmur of the TV.

"No, what?" she replied, keeping an ear tuned to Ben's splashing in the tub.

Matt appeared and leaned against the doorjamb, watching her. "Lloyd Whitney died."

"Oh?" she said, tearing lettuce into the salad bowl. "Who was he?"

Matt stared at her for a moment. "Lloyd Harmon Whitney, the Arizona real-estate tycoon."

"Oh, yeah. Wasn't he sort of a Howard Hughes type?" She sliced the last of the cucumber, and thrust the bowl into Matt's hands. "Just put this on the table. I've got to get Ben out of that tub and into his pajamas. We'll eat in a couple of minutes."

Matt stood in the doorway, a thoughtful expression on his face. Then he shrugged and turned away.

After dinner, Matt offered to help with the clearing up. He carried the plates into the kitchen as Ben, hanging on Vicky's arm, said, "Mom, it's time for a story."

Vicky sighed. "In a minute, honey, as soon as I'm finished here."

"Want me to read you a story, Ben?" Matt asked.

Vicky shot him a grateful look. "Would you? That would be great."

"'Three Little Pigs'!" Ben shouted as he charged out to the living room.

Matt grinned at Vicky and followed him.

Over the sound of the running water, Vicky soon heard a deep voice: "I'll huff and I'll puff and I'll *blow* your house down!" It was answered by Ben's high-pitched giggle. Finishing up at the sink, she turned to put on a pot of coffee and was surprised to hear Matt's voice saying, "Someone's been eating my porridge," and Ben shrieking, "It was Goldilocks!"

Oh dear, she thought, two stories. She whipped down the hall to her bedroom and quickly ran a comb through her hair. She'd better rescue Matt. Entering the living room, she paused. Matt's dark head was bent close to Ben's carrot-top as the two of them sat together, turning the pages. This is good for Ben, she thought. Just then her ears registered Matt's words. "I think I can, I think I can," he chanted. Another story!

She crossed the room and sat on Ben's other side while Matt brought *The Little Engine That Could* over the hill. At the end of the story, she said, "Ben, that's all for tonight. Matt was very kind to read three stories—now you're off to bed."

When Vicky returned to the living room, she said with an embarrassed laugh, "Thanks. That was above and beyond."

"I enjoyed it," Matt said. "He's a great kid. You're doing a wonderful job. What does he do all day while you're at work?"

Vicky told him about Ben's nursery school. A little surprised at his interest, she described the program and explained about Mrs. Garfield. "I don't know what I'd do without her," she concluded.

"It must be terrific, living so near the beach," said Matt. "Ben's so well coordinated, I'll bet he swims like a fish."

"No, not yet," Vicky laughed. "He loves the water, but he just splashes around in it so far. I really have to keep an eye on him, especially around pools. I always make him wear his life jacket."

Matt nodded thoughtfully. Then he said, "I guess I'd better get going. I've imposed on you long enough."

36

"Where are you staying?" asked Vicky.

"In my van. I found a good place to camp up near Malibu, so I think I'll stay around for a while. Can I take you and Ben out for dinner some other night?"

Vicky smiled. "I know Ben would like that. Give me a call."

At the door, Matt turned to her. Standing so close to him, she realized suddenly how tall and powerful he was.

"I'm really sorry about Tom," he said. "Even more sorry, now that I've met Ben." His tone was so strange that Vicky didn't know how to respond. She shut the door behind him and leaned against it with a puzzled frown.

Vicky looked up from her potter's wheel. Ben seemed happy with his bits of clay. He was carefully rolling them up into balls and then pressing them flat with his thumbs. She was glad he was old enough now to come with her; it was fun for both of them, and she found it relaxing and fulfilling to create something with her hands. The inexpensive monthly membership fee allowed her to use all the equipment and to come and go whenever she liked. She often came down for an hour or so, early in the evening after work.

Vicky began drawing up the sides of the bowl she was shaping. I'm getting much better at this, she thought as her skilled fingers evened the walls of the bowl. Maybe I should see about an advanced class. I wonder if they have a class for children too.

A slight blond woman stood mixing glazes at the other end of the table Ben was working on. She disappeared and then returned, carefully carrying two stemmed goblets from the firing shelf. Setting them down gently, she went back for the other two she'd made. Ben slipped off his chair and moved closer to watch as she began applying the glaze.

"Careful, Ben," Vicky called. "Don't get in Andrea's way—those things are fragile."

"Oh, he's okay," Andrea reassured her, then said to Ben, "As soon as I finish this, I'll help you make something. What would you like to make?"

A short while later, Vicky walked over to find Andrea and Ben busily rolling long ropes of clay between their palms.

"Look, Mom, we're making worms," Ben said proudly.

"Keep them as even as you can, Ben," Andrea cautioned. "When we have enough, we'll coil them into a basket shape."

Vicky smiled at them, and returned to her wheel. Under her sure touch, the piece she was working on took on a classically graceful shape. When she was satisfied, she cut it from the wheel and carried it on its board to the firing shelf. After cleaning up her workspace and washing her hands at the big old-fashioned sink, Vicky went to collect her son.

"I made a clay basket," Ben informed her. "Andrea says I can cook it in the kiln."

Andrea was smoothing the inside of the basket with her wet fingers. "I think it will come out just fine," she replied to Vicky's questioning look.

"It's beautiful. Ben!" Vicky exclaimed. "Next time we come, I'll help you glaze it." She turned to Andrea. "Thanks a lot."

Andrea laughed. "I had fun. It's a long time since I made one of those coiled numbers."

She took the little basket over to the firing shelf

while Vicky helped Ben wash his clay-covered hands. As they walked toward the door, Vicky waved to Andrea and called, "See you soon."

Ben waved too. "'Bye!" Looking up at Vicky, he confided in the same loud voice, "I like Andrea a lot, Mom—she's neat."

Taking his hand, Vicky said, "I'm glad you had fun."

Vicky threaded her little red beetle through the quiet Venice streets. She loved this area. Despite the proliferation of sterile apartment complexes in Los Angeles's West Side, Venice had managed to retain its slightly seedy charm. Spanish-style bungalows snuggled up to Victorian gingerbread monsters on the narrow lots. And the salt air from the ocean a few blocks away seemed to be the perfect tonic for flowers of all kinds. Dahlias, snapdragons, phlox, and climbing roses coexisted in harmony with exotic tropicals like bird-of-paradise and hibiscus. When the marina just to the south had opened in the early sixties, developers had cast covetous eyes on Venice, with its prime location. Dredgers had been all set to clean up and enlarge the network of tiny earth-walled canals that gave Venice its name. Real-estate operators bought everything they could, planning to raze the shabby old buildings and erect high-priced luxury housing. But the disparate community of pensioners on social security, beach bums, and aging hippies had pulled together to halt the so-called progress, and so far they had managed to hold the developers at bay. It would be a shame, Vicky thought, if the steel-and-concrete people had their way and turned Venice into another characterless playground for the rich.

Vicky drew up at the stop sign and glanced in her

rearview mirror as a car turned on its lights and pulled out of the line of parked vehicles behind her. Her right-turn signal clicking, she edged slowly into the intersection. Then, in amazement, she watched the car's lights barreling up on her tail. He's not going to stop! she realized. Gripping the steering wheel in alarm, she pressed harder on the accelerator to try and get out of his way. But at the last possible moment, the big green station wagon pulled to the left, passing her, and then cut sharply right. Vicky slammed on the brakes, and the larger car sliced across in front of her, missing her bumper by just inches.

The station wagon roared away as Vicky turned quickly to Ben. "Are you okay, honey?"

"Yeah," he answered, pushing himself firmly back in the passenger seat.

The VW had stalled. Realizing that she was still sitting in the right-hand lane, Vicky hastily started the engine. As she drove off, she muttered under her breath, "Crazy drivers! He ought to lose his license."

Her red beetle continued north on Pacific Avenue. By the time she braked for the light at Rose, Ben was eagerly describing the outing his school group would take the next day. The four-lane street was nearly empty. Ahead of her, deep crimson slashed across the sky in the sunset's afterglow.

The light changed, and Vicky let in the clutch. She moved briskly along, eager to get home. Suddenly a big square car backed at high speed out of a sidestreet onto Pacific, directly in her path. Vicky had no choice. Cutting the wheel sharply, she swerved across the double yellow line into the oncoming lane.

That's the same car! her mind told her, while her hands fought the wheel. Coming at her was an old pickup truck. Vicky threw the VW into a sliding skid, trying to get back into her lane. But the station wagon came up fast on her right, preventing her from moving over. The pickup, its horn blaring, veered and flashed by on her left, its wheels just clearing the far curb.

Vicky slowed and the station wagon shot ahead, its taillights disappearing in the gathering dusk. White-faced and shaking, she pulled at last into the far right lane. Ben's eyes were enormous as he looked at her.

"It's okay, honey," she said, her voice trembling. "It's okay now." She'd been angry the first time, but now she was getting scared. Her only thought was to get home.

As she crossed Pico, the brightly lit streets of Santa Monica reassured her. Cars came and went in the motel parking lots. Passing the pier, she saw tourists and locals enjoying a stroll in the evening air. She stayed on Ocean Avenue, but after the Miramar, the neon lights were behind her. Not much farther, she thought.

Her faithful beetle purred along at a steady thirty miles per hour, and a few impatient types passed her in the fast lane. Then, with a sinking heart, she saw a pair of headlights moving up fast behind her. It was the green station wagon.

Vicky didn't know what to do. She couldn't possibly outrun the larger car's heavy engine and superior horsepower. If she turned into a sidestreet, she'd be even more isolated. Bracing herself, she said in a strained voice, "Ben, get down on the floor, right away."

Expecting the station wagon to ram her from behind, Vicky wasn't prepared for what happened next. The big green car shot out alongside her as though to pass, then swung violently in front of her, forcing her into the curb. She was slammed against the steering wheel as the VW's wheels hit the concrete with a sickening jolt.

Dazed, Vicky heard the screech of brakes as the station wagon stopped about fifty yards ahead. Vicky watched in horror as the white reversing lights sped toward her. She screamed, "Stay down, Ben!" Desperately she tried to reverse her own car, hoping to lessen the impact of the inevitable crash.

Loud, insistent honking broke through her panicky concentration. A gleaming white Cadillac glided massively around her and drew into the curb. Looking up, she saw the station wagon leap forward, swing right on San Vicente, and vanish.

The Cadillac's door opened and a well-dressed, gray-haired man got out. By this time, Ben had both of his arms wrapped tightly around Vicky's neck. He was sobbing and crying "Mommy, Mommy," over and over. She did her best to calm him as the Cadillac's driver approached her car.

"Are you all right? I saw what happened." As he spoke, he opened her door and helped her clamber out, with Ben still clinging to her neck.

"I guess so," Vicky answered weakly.

After a close look at her, he said with authority, "Just sit down over here on the curb. Is the boy all right? Let's have a look."

Grateful for the man's supporting arm, Vicky sank to the curb and kissed Ben's pale cheek. She gently loosened his small arms and held him on her lap. A large lump was already forming over his right eye, and a little blood was oozing from an ugly bruise at his hairline.

"Do you want me to take you to a hospital?"

After another look at Ben's face, Vicky shook her head. "I'm pretty sure he's okay—these are just bruises. I'd really rather go home."

He nodded in agreement. "Probably best to get him home and into bed. Do you have far to go?"

"No, no," Vicky said quickly. "That's all right."

He walked over to the VW and bent to inspect the tires and front end. "Looks like your car's okay. You're pretty lucky—I guess these things are indestructible." Straightening again, he went on, "I don't suppose you got that lunatic's license number."

"No."

"That's too bad. But you really should report him anyway. You can never tell, maybe they'll catch him and then they can throw the book at him. These idiots shouldn't be allowed on the road."

"No, please," Vicky said tiredly. "I don't think I can go through all that. I just want to get home."

He looked at her in surprise. "You're not going to report it?" Then, taking in her clay-stained Levi's, her Newport Jazz Festival T-shirt, and her rubber thong sandals, his tone cooled. "Well, it's up to you."

Oh God, Vicky thought, now he thinks I'm some sort of hippie who just had a fight with her boyfriend. Aloud she said, "I can't begin to thank you. I don't know what would have happened if you hadn't come along."

With a dismissing wave, he said, "As long as you're okay. I'll just wait and make sure your car will start."

Wearily, Vicky stood up and carried Ben to the car. Settling him carefully in the front seat, she climbed in and turned the key in the ignition. The little car started right up. As she backed away from the curb, she gave her rescuer a wave, and then started slowly toward home.

An hour later, Vicky collapsed thankfully into bed. She was almost too spent to think. How had she managed to cross the path of that maniac driver? Did he just like to bully smaller cars, or had she unknowingly done something to set him off? At least neither she nor Ben had been badly injured. She turned over, trying to erase the image of the speeding car bearing down on her. An involuntary shiver of fear ran through her.

—Could it have happened to anyone in a red VW, or was he lying in wait for me?

"What a glorious day!" Vicky said, turning her face up to the sun. "You must have brought good weather with you, Matt."

"So this is what beach living is all about." Matt smiled and stepped quickly out of the path of two teenaged girls clad in skimpy bikinis, skating arm-in-arm along the beachfront walk. Everyone seemed to be on roller skates, gliding past sidewalk cafes, open-air galleries, and vendors of handcrafted jewelry.

The three of them strolled slowly up Ocean Front Walk, the broad beach stretching away to their left.

"Well," Vicky said mischievously, "we're almost to Muscle Beach." Matt gave her an inquiring look and she added, "Wait and see." A few more yards and there it was: a small fenced enclosure crowded with every imaginable kind of weightlifting and muscle-building equipment. Twenty or more men were working out—old and young, black and white, but all with the heavy musculature and sweaty sheen of the true believer.

Matt stared in amazement, and then turned to Vicky. "Portland was never like this! Let's stop and watch."

Ben tugged at Vicky's hand. "Mom, can I go to the playground?"

"Go ahead," she replied. "Matt and I will be along in a few minutes." She watched him run up the walk and into the playground a few yards from where she stood.

His eyes glued to a bronzed, elderly athlete lifting barbells with astonishing ease, Matt asked Vicky, "Is this a special contest today?"

"Oh no, they're here working out every day, rain or shine. It's a weightlifting club. All these guys are probably regulars."

"Unbelievable," said Matt, shaking his head.

"I know—that's Venice Beach. Come on, let's go get Ben."

They walked over to the playground. It was completely deserted. Vicky looked around frantically; Ben wasn't on the sidewalk, either. Vicky's hand flew to her throat. "Oh no!" Then she shouted, "Ben? Ben! Where are you?"

Matt put a hand on her arm. "Take it easy, he can't have gone very far."

Ignoring him, Vicky rushed back the way they had come, past the paddle-tennis courts. And there was Ben, his face pushed up against the fence, watching a game.

"Ben! Come here this minute!" In her relief, she spoke sharply. "You were supposed to be in the playground. You can't just wander off without telling me. If you can't behave, we won't be able to come here anymore."

Ben looked crushed. He'd only gone a few steps from the playground. Quickly he trotted to Vicky's side and put his hand in hers. Vicky, intent on her son, never noticed Matt's look of surprised disapproval.

By the time they reached the Pavilion, Vicky's overreaction had faded. The three of them wandered around the grassy space. Throngs of people were gathered to gawk or participate in the bouncing folk dances, the spectacular Frisbee competition, and the demonstrations of belly dancing and hypnotism. Over it all sounded the insistent rhythms of bongo drums. Overhead floated a fantastic array of elaborate kites, held aloft by the constant ocean breeze. Dragons, fish, and butterflies in vivid purples and reds swooped over box kites of intricate design. There were even whole families of kites on one string. Ben was entranced. Without a word, he flopped down on the warm sand and stared up at the soaring spectacle. Matt and Vicky grinned at one another.

"He's got the right idea," Matt said. The two of them stretched out on the sand beside Ben and gazed upward.

Later, they sat eating hamburgers in the Front Walk. Their table by the railing turned out to be a perfect spot from which to watch the ever-changing kaleidoscope of the Venice Fair. As soon as Ben finished his food, he started fidgeting in his seat. It was obvious that he was tired of sitting still. Besides, there were too many things to see and do. Several stray dogs mooched by to beg for handouts.

"Mom, can I go out and pet that dog?"

"Okay, honey, but don't go far." As he slipped down

from the chair and started away, she caught his arms and pulled him around to face her, imprisoning his small body between her bare knees. "Now listen to me, Ben. You can go as far as the grass and no farther. And stay in front of this restaurant—don't go past the end of the railing on either side. Understand?"

"Okay, Mom." He squirmed away and she watched after him, an anxious frown clouding her face.

"Aren't you being a little heavy?" Matt asked. "What could happen to him here?"

"Maybe you're right." Vicky paused. "But so many strange things have been happening, I guess I'm a little nervous."

"What kind of strange things?" he asked.

"Well," she said with a little laugh, "you'll probably think I'm crazy, but..."

She started with her problem with the persistent, silent phone calls, and went on to tell him about Ben's near miss with his tricycle out in the street. Matt looked tolerant, but when she described the terrifying trip home from the pottery studio, his expression changed to one of concern.

"And then I started thinking. A couple of weeks ago, some man called and said he was from the Dewitt Modeling Agency. He told me someone had recommended Ben for child modeling, and asked me to send him a recent picture of Ben. He gave me a post office box number to send it to. At first I thought it was one of those come-ons, but he swore it was absolutely free and there was no obligation. So I said I'd do it; after all, the Dewitt Agency is pretty well known. But after I hung up, I had a funny feeling about it, so I decided to call him back and find out exactly how he got Ben's name. I looked them up in the phone book and called back. But there was no one there by that name. I talked to some lady in the children's division, and she said they'd never heard of me, and besides, they never use post office boxes."

Matt leaned back in his chair. "Well, that's a little peculiar, but you didn't send the picture."

"I know," said Vicky, "but I'm such a fool. He asked me all these questions about Ben, and I went ahead and told him. Don't you see? He already had my address and phone number." She heard her voice rising shrilly, and broke off. "I don't know what it was all about," she went on more calmly. "I didn't really think much about it, but when all these other things started happening, I began to wonder." She took a sip of coffee and then said with a half-laugh, "Or do I just sound totally crazy?"

Matt reached across the table. His strong fingers felt warm and reassuring as he covered her hand with his. "I can see how all these things coming together would be upsetting. But if you look at each one on its own, they're not so serious. I think you've just had a string of unpleasant coincidences."

"I hope you're right," Vicky said. Nervously she pulled her hand away and adjusted her sunglasses. "Anyway, it's been a relief to talk to you. I haven't told anyone else about it."

Chapter 3

Driving along the familiar route to work, Vicky half-listened to the radio. She was pleased that there seemed to be no major tie-ups in front of her and traffic was moving fairly well. She caught the tail end of a singing commercial: "Sav-On Drug Stores, Sav-On Drug Stores." That reminds me, she thought, I must stop and get toothpaste. And there was something else—was it Band-Aids? The radio droned on in the background as her thoughts drifted to the work she had planned for the morning.

—I hope I can get away early—it's such a super day. Wonder how Matt's doing. It must be hard to be at the beach and get any work done. I'll have to be sure and ask him this evening how the book is coming along.

He certainly is an attractive man—just like the old cliche, tall, dark, and handsome. But he's so different from Tom. It's hard to imagine them rooming together.

She remembered the first time she'd met Tom. Through an odd chain of circumstances, she'd been invited to a glittering Hollywood party at the home of the producer Huavos Fried. She'd felt like the country cousin among all those famous and gorgeously attired film people. And there was Tom, with a brash self-confidence that bordered on arrogance but insured that he was never without an audience. Vicky had been astonished when he had slid his arm around her waist and whispered in her ear, "The prettiest girl at the dance and all alone! Let me show you where they hid the good champagne."

She laughed at the memory. Matt would never do anything like that, but his quiet strength had its own appeal. I'm glad he called, she thought. I wonder how long he'll stay here? He's obviously footloose and fancy-free—not the kind I'd want to get involved with, even if I were ready to get involved with someone, which I'm not.

The Ford in front of her slowed abruptly. As it came to a stop, its left blinker flashed on. "Damn!" Vicky muttered. At last she managed to pull around the immobile car and get back into the flow of traffic. The radio was just finishing a commercial for Forest Lawn.

"... And now for today's business news. Quite a legal battle seems to be shaping up over real-estate entrepreneur Lloyd Harmon Whitney's estate. Since his father's recent death, Whitney Enterprises has been in the hands of Charles Whitney, the younger son. But it now appears that the multimillionaire's will leaves the controlling interest to his elder son, Lloyd Thomas

Whitney. Here's more from Mary Jane Kearny in Phoenix."

"Well, Jim, this is turning out to be a real mystery. About ten years ago, Lloyd Thomas Whitney broke off contact with his family, and no one around here has seen him since then. It was quite a shock when the will was opened. Efforts to locate Lloyd Junior have so far been unsuccessful. And we understand that Charles Whitney will try to move to have his brother declared legally dead."

"Boy, sounds like Perry Mason in real life down there. That'll be a long, drawn out legal proceeding."

"Yes, it will, Jim. But of course, Charles may decide in the meantime to contest the will. We'll just have to wait and see."

"Thanks, Mary Jane. And now the stock market. Trading this morning..."

Vicky turned onto the Fox parking lot. As she got out of her car she smiled wryly.

—The rich certainly have a different set of problems from the rest of us.

She walked across the lot toward her building, enjoying the sun as she detoured around a group of ten-foot-tall plaster-of-paris nude statues.

—Are they going to shoot a Roman epic? Tomorrow it'll probably be chariots!

She'd learned by this time never to be surprised at the odd props scattered all over the studio lot. "Hi, Cindy!" she called, as she opened the door to her office.

Mrs. Garfield rubbed at a stubborn spot on the window-pane and then stood back for a critical look. Certainly makes a difference, she thought. I think I might just get these front windows all done before I have to leave.

She squirted Windex on the next pane. Just as she attacked it with her cloth, the phone rang.

—Wouldn't you know.

She picked it up on the third ring. "Yes?"

"Is that Mrs. Garfield?"

"Sure is."

The man's voice was businesslike. "I'm calling from the Meadowlark Nursery School. Mrs. Hunter asked us to let you know she'll be picking Ben up at school today."

Mrs. Garfield said in surprise, "She didn't mention it to me."

"That's why she asked us to call. She forgot about it until just now, and she was rushing to a meeting. I think she's taking him to get new shoes."

"Oh. So she doesn't want me to come over at all this afternoon?"

"That's right. She said she'd call you tonight."

"Well. Thanks for calling, then." She hung up and went back to her windows. Might as well try to get the whole house done, as long as she had the whole afternoon to herself.

At ten minutes after one, the Meadowlark minibus turned into Seaview Avenue and stopped at number 19. The door opened and Ben jumped out. "'Bye!" he yelled.

"'Bye!" answered a chorus of young voices as the driver waved and pulled away.

Ben pushed through the open gate and ran up to the front door. They always played this game; Mrs. Garfield tried to open the front door before Ben got to the top step. Today Ben won. The door didn't open.

He waited a few moments, a gleeful smile on his face. Then he tried to turn the doorknob, but it was locked.

"Hello, Ben." A man appeared around the side of the house.

"Who are you?" Ben asked.

"I'm a friend of Mrs. Garfield's," the man said easily. "She can't come today and she asked me to take care of you. We're going to go to my house and play in the backyard."

"Where is your house?"

"A couple of blocks away—we'll walk over there." The man held out his hand. "Let's go."

Ben refused his outstretched hand, but skipped down the steps and followed the man out the gate.

They walked nearly three blocks up the hill. The houses here looked prosperous and well-cared-for, screened from one another by the thick trees and sloping ground of the canyon. They turned in the driveway of an angular contemporary redwood house, nestled among tall eucalyptus and pines. Heavy drapes were drawn closely across its numerous large windows and sliding glass doors.

Ben followed the man past the empty garage and through the gate at the side of the house. The tall, woven-redwood fence enclosed the cleverly landscaped yard whose plantings echoed the natural beauty of the canyon. A brick patio surrounded a sparkling free-form swimming pool.

Ben looked around. The two of them were alone.

"Some other kids will be here after a while," the man told him. "You can all go swimming."

"But I didn't bring my swimsuit," Ben began.

"That's okay, you can swim in those shorts you have on. I'll just help you off with that T-shirt."

Ben put up his arms obediently, and the man pulled the shirt over his head.

"There are some pool toys over there; choose whatever you want to play with." As Ben started toward the open cabanas, the man added. "You can go ahead and swim. I just have to make a phone call."

He walked quickly to the gate. Slipping out, he reached up to secure the high latch behind him.

Vicky looked up from her desk as Cindy poked her head in the door.

"Vicky, honey!" Cindy exclaimed. "Didn't you go to lunch?"

"No, I decided to stay here and finish this pile of work," Vicky replied. "I'm going to go home early—the rest of this is stuff I can read at home."

Cindy sighed enviously. "Surely wish I had a job like that. An afternoon at the beach sounds just fine."

Laughing, Vicky said, "Sounds fine to me, too, but I'll be chained to my desk with the phone off the hook."

"Well, see y'all tomorrow, then. Don't overstrain your big brown eyes with all that reading."

As Cindy turned away with a wave, Vicky stuffed three more fat scripts into her already bulging canvas tote. She switched off her desk lamp and went out.

Zipping down San Vicente, Vicky thought, maybe I should run into the drugstore now and pick up that toothpaste. She slowed down and moved over to the right lane. No, I think we've got enough till the weekend—I'd rather get home and have some time with Ben before dinner.

She pulled into her driveway and maneuvered the

little car into the garage between her bicycle and a bag of peat moss. Lugging her papers, she went in the back door. "Hi, I'm home!"

No one answered as she walked through to her desk, which was stuck in one corner of the dining area, and dumped the stack of scripts. They must have gone to the beach, she decided. I'll make some coffee, and then I'll get to work.

Waiting for the water to boil, Vicky went into her room and changed into shorts and a loose shirt. I'll just get this laundry done now, she said to herself, emptying her own hamper. She carried the laundry basket into Ben's room and collected his dirty clothes. Looking under the bed for stray socks, she found a T-shirt and Ben's swimsuit.

—Funny, Mrs. Garfield didn't have him change. But maybe they went to the park.

Loading the washing machine, she was about to turn away when she saw Ben's sand pail and shovel; she'd put them there on the dryer the other day, and had never gotten around to moving them.

—I guess they didn't go to the park after all—Ben would have wanted his pail for the sandbox. Maybe I should call and see if they're at Mrs. Garfield's house. I'll just tell her I'm home.

Vicky dialed the familiar number and got a busy signal. She poured herself some coffee and went to her desk, clearing a space and opening the first of the scripts. She read a page or two, then reached for the phone and tried the number again. Mrs. Garfield answered promptly.

"Hi, Mrs. Garfield, it's Vicky. I'm home early—just wanted to let you know."

"Oh. So should I come over now?"

"No, that's all right, I have some work to do. About three o'clock will be fine."

Mrs. Garfield sounded a little surprised. "Okay. How are the new shoes?"

"What?" It was Vicky's turn to be surprised.

Mrs. Garfield explained, "I just wondered if you got him those Snoopy sneakers he's been asking for."

Vicky laughed. "Oh no. I just got him new shoes a couple of weeks ago."

"But I thought—" Mrs. Garfield paused. "Weren't you getting him new shoes today?"

"No," Vicky said patiently. "Besides, I couldn't very well buy shoes for Ben without having him along."

With an audible gasp, Mrs. Garfield asked, "But isn't Ben with you?"

Vicky's knuckles whitened on the receiver. Striving to keep her voice even, she said, "No, he isn't, Mrs. Garfield. Didn't you meet him when he came home from school?"

"Why, no. The man from his school said you were going to pick him up there."

"Oh my God." Vicky felt as if she couldn't breathe. As calmly as she could, she said, "Tell me exactly what this man said."

Mrs. Garfield eagerly related the entire conversation. As she reached the end, Vicky cut her off. "I see. Something's gone wrong. I'll talk to you later."

Breaking the connection, she debated what to do next. Could there have been some mix-up at the school? Quickly she dialed and waited while the phone rang and rang, willing someone to answer. At last she heard a youthful voice: "Hello, Meadowlark School."

"This is Mrs. Hunter. Is my son Ben still there, by any chance? He's got red hair and—"

"Oh, I know who Ben is," the girl interrupted. "But all the kids are gone. I'm sure he got on the bus with the rest of them. There's no one here but me." She paused, then added, "Is anything wrong?"

Vicky said distractedly, "I don't know... thanks, goodbye."

She stood gnawing her knuckle. What if Ben had come home and, finding no one there, started fooling around outside? Maybe he had hurt himself—he could be lying somewhere unconscious, unable to call out for help. Vicky ran out the back door, calling his name. He wasn't in the yard, there was nothing that could be concealing a small body. The garage? Past the car, she made her way to the back. The shelves were packed solid with storage boxes and trunks full of books and papers—no way he could have wriggled between them. But there was a pile of empty cartons on the floor. She pulled them away from the wall, but he wasn't inside or behind any of them.

Knowing it was futile, she ran out of the garage and around to its other side. Walking along the thick bushes there, she parted them carefully and peered in. But he wouldn't be here; he had always been a bit scared of this dark overgrown area. With a sinking heart, she faced the fact that he was gone.

She returned to the house and found the police emergency number. When the desk sergeant answered, she said in a rush, "I want to report a missing child." She explained everything that had happened, nearly crying with frustration at his methodical slowness.

At last he said, "Stay right where you are, ma'am. We'll have someone there right away."

Her voice breaking, Vicky said, "Please hurry."

She couldn't sit still. Her whole body felt wired, as

charges of adrenalin pumped through her system. Every primitive instinct was driving her to go out and find her lost child, but she had to wait for the police. She paced frantically through the house. Pictures! They'd said they needed photographs of Ben. At least she could do that.

She raced back to her desk and pulled out the drawer. There were some photos in here somewhere from the last roll she'd taken. Scrabbling furiously through the heap of papers, she snatched up a yellow photo envelope. Inside were several shots of Ben at the beach, hamming for the camera, and on his tricycle in front of the house. She shook them out on the coffee table. Then, hearing a car, she rushed to the front door and flung it open. There was Matt's blue van.

"Matt! Thank God you're here!" She threw herself down the steps. Matt took one look at her wild eyes and pale face. In three quick strides, he reached her and caught her arm.

"Vicky, what's wrong?"

"It's Ben! He's gone, he didn't come home from school, someone's got him!" She was babbling incoherently.

He led her into the house and, pushing her gently down on the couch, said, "Slow down. Tell me what's going on."

Vicky gulped convulsively and began. When he had sorted out her story, Matt said. "The police are right, you've got to stay here. What if Ben wanders home on his own?"

The tears welled up in Vicky's eyes as she stared at him helplessly. Taking her hands, he went on, "Let's think about this. If he got on the school bus, he must have been dropped off at home. So he may not have gotten very far. I'm going to go out and look for him."

She nodded, not trusting herself to speak.

"Look, Vicky, it may not be as bad as you think." He stood up. "I'll be in touch."

He left, and Vicky buried her face in her hands. Long, shuddering sobs racked her body as she gave way to her fear.

A loud knocking roused her. Wiping her eyes with one hand, she opened the door for the two uniformed police officers.

"Mrs. Hunter?" said the big, burly black man. "I'm Officer Robinson. And this is Officer Rosales." He indicated the dark-haired young woman beside him. "We have a report of a missing child. Has your son returned?"

"No," Vicky said shakily. "Please come in."

Once again she explained what had happened, while Officer Robinson made rapid notes.

"I see," he said. "And you've looked around the property?"

Vicky nodded vigorously. "I've looked everywhere."

"Right, ma'am." Turning to Rosales, he said. "Take a look around and then come back here." To Vicky, he went on, "Do you have a recent snapshot of the boy?"

Vicky indicated the photos on the coffee table. "Take what you need."

In reply to his quick questions, she supplied the details that would enable the police to recognize Ben.

"Is there anyone else who could have picked the boy up? How about his father?"

"My husband is dead." Vicky said flatly.

"Any other relatives in the area?" As Vicky shook her head, he continued, "Or maybe a boyfriend?"

"No, there's no one," she told him impatiently.

Officer Rosales came back into the room and shook her head slightly at her partner. The tall policeman snapped his notebook shut and said, "Right, ma'am. I'll call this in. Officer Rosales here will get started on the phone; she'll need the numbers of your sitter and the school."

He went outside to the black-and-white police cruiser parked at the curb. The young woman picked up the phone and began dialing the first number on Vicky's hastily scribbled list.

"Mrs. Garfield? This is Officer Rosales of the LAPD..."

Feeling useless, Vicky went to the windows and peered out. The policeman was leaning on the open door of the squad car. She saw his lips move as he spoke into the microphone in his hand.

"That's right. The drainage canal is right alongside the property. I'll drop down in there and start checking it out. Rosales can take the immediate house-to-house."

The microphone crackled. "Ten-four. I'll send a car to assist."

"Ten-four." Robinson replaced the microphone and headed back into the house.

Rosales looked up from the telephone. "I've got that bus driver's name and number now."

"Right, get that checked first. Then you can start knocking on doors." The policewoman opened her mouth to speak, then caught her partner's warning look. "They're sending another car," he added, and turned to leave.

Vicky intercepted him, her anguished eyes pleading.

"Try not to worry, ma'am," he told her gently, then he was gone.

She hovered irresolutely in the doorway, listening to Rosales's half of the phone conversation.

"So you didn't see anyone, inside or outside." She paused. "All right, thank you, Mr. Sanzo. If you think of anything else, please call this number—814-2727—and ask for Sergeant Myers."

Hanging up, she turned to Vicky. "It looks like your son was dropped off at home, Mrs. Hunter, so we'll be starting on a search of the immediate area."

"Can't I help? I've got to do something," Vicky said in a tightly controlled voice.

"No," the policewoman said. She sounded sympathetic. "I know it's hard, but the best thing for you to do is stay right here. Someone may call, or even find your son and bring him home. We'll be checking back here from time to time." With an understanding smile, she went out. Vicky was alone.

She moved nervously to the window again, and looked out. Nothing seemed to be happening, though she knew the police were working as fast as they could. She longed to leave the confines of the house and take an active role in the search. Pacing distractedly toward the telephone, she thought, I need to talk to someone. But most of her friends would be at work. Maybe she could ask Cindy to come; under that flighty manner, Vicky knew there was a core of good sense and genuine concern. She reached for the phone and then froze.

—I can't tie up the phone—what if someone calls?

She picked up her coffee cup and drank thirstily, hardly noticing that the liquid was bitter and cold. Putting the cup down absently, Vicky shivered. She hugged herself and fidgeted again through the living room. Suddenly, a movement outside the window caught her eye.

Mrs. Garfield bustled up the front walk. "Oh, Mrs. Hunter, you poor thing!" she breathed as she came in the house. "I just had to come over and see if you've heard anything about Ben." One look at Vicky's face told her that there had been no news. "That sweet little boy. Whoever would do such a thing? I just can't imagine what happened. As soon as I heard, I said to myself, 'I should have asked that man his name.' But who would have thought it was some sort of prank? I mean, he sounded just like a regular person. But I can't help blaming myself." Vicky tried to say something reassuring, but Mrs. Garfield plowed on, hardly pausing to take a breath, "Good thing you got the police. I always say, when you're in trouble, call a policeman. After all, that's what they're there for." She registered Vicky's drawn look of tension. "Oh, just listen to me rattling on when you look like you're ready to collapse. Why don't you sit down and I'll brew you a nice, soothing cup of tea. No sense you falling apart yet. I always say, no news is good news."

Vicky put up her hand to protest. "No, really, don't bother."

"No bother. I mean, I came over to help, after all. And there has to be something I can do."

Vicky seized on this opening. "There *is* something you can do. Stay right here in the house. I've just got to get out and look for him myself. But someone has to be here in case anything happens."

"I understand just how you feel. You go on ahead. I'll be right here."

Vicky headed for the door. "Now, if anyone calls,

take a message. The police number is on that pad. But be sure not to tie up the phone."

"Of course not. I know better than that! Don't worry, I'll take care of everything." As Vicky opened the door, Mrs. Garfield added, "Mrs. Hunter?" Vicky turned. "I'll be praying for you and little Ben."

"Thank you." Vicky smiled wanly as she closed the door.

On the sidewalk, Vicky looked up and down the street. Officer Rosales was standing on a porch a few houses away, toward Entrada. She was talking to a young man with a blond ponytail. Quickly, Vicky turned and walked in the other direction.

Ben knelt on the brick patio, rolling a shuffleboard disk on its edge. Scattered around him were other shuffleboard disks, an inflated porpoise from Marineland, a basketball hoop with its white styrofoam flotation collar, and several pool balls. The disk hit a protruding edge of brick and fell over. Bored with that game, Ben looked around. A bright orange-and-white striped beach ball caught his interest. He stood and went to pick it up. He bounced the ball several times on the bricks. It flew out of his grasp and rolled toward the pool. Ben watched it go, then, distracted by a noise, he looked over toward the gate.

"Mommy?" he called hopefully.

I wonder if he could somehow have gone up to the park, Vicky said to herself. If he had found no one at home, he might have wandered up there. He certainly knew the way. She crossed West Channel and headed up into the canyon. Breaking into a run, she followed the tree-shaded, winding roadway. She cut over onto another of the narrow roads, and moved to the side for a passing car.

As she reached the park, Vicky started to call, "Ben? Ben?" A couple of women playing tennis looked annoyed when she interrupted their game. "Have you seen a little red-haired boy?" Vicky asked them. "He's only three and a half, and he's missing!"

The women's looks softened, but they shook their heads. He hadn't been by there.

Several older children were playing near the swings. Vicky ran over to them. "Have you seen my little boy? Ben? He's about this tall and has red hair." She held out her hand below waist level and waited hopefully. The kids looked at one another and shrugged their shoulders.

One of them said, "We haven't seen him. Is he lost?"

"Yes, he is," said Vicky. "If you see him, please keep him here. I'll be back."

"Okay," said the girl who seemed to be their leader. They were eager to help, but Vicky knew there was little chance they would find him.

Vicky looked once more around the park, checking the heavily padlocked equipment shed and behind the large trees, even though she felt sure Ben wasn't playing hide-and-seek with her. Not knowing what else to do, she went back to the road and continued on up into the canyon.

The entire hillside was covered with a maze of little roads going off at peculiar angles, many of them dead-ending after a few curving blocks. It was all overgrown and rustic. People up here paid a high price for privacy. How could she ever find Ben if he'd become lost and was just wandering around? she thought with despair. A man pulled into the driveway nearest her. As he got out of his car, Vicky asked, "Have you seen a little redheaded boy?" He stared at her, then shook his head.

Vicky kept walking, choosing which street to follow at random, since there was no way of guessing which one a small boy might take. Every now and then she called, "Ben? Ben!" Sometimes the tall trees and sloping ground deadened her voice, and at other times she heard herself echoed oddly. She saw almost no one. At midafternoon, residents here were either at work or out shopping.

There was an old pickup truck parked in front of one of the houses. A man came around the side, hosing down the driveway. Vicky raised her voice over the sound of running water. "Have you seen a little boy with red hair?"

The man looked up and saw her. Kinking the hose to stop the flow of water, he smiled shyly at Vicky and walked down the driveway toward her. "A little boy?" she repeated, holding out her hand to indicate Ben's size. "Red hair?" He kept smiling, but his blank expression told her that he understood no English. She searched her mind for the Spanish words. *"Niño? Rojo..."* She couldn't think of the word for "hair." Vicky pointed to her own hair and then to a mass of red geraniums in giant pots. *"Rojo,"* she repeated.

The gardener's brown eyes were sympathetic. He seemed to understand. *"No, Señora. No niño aquî,"* he said sadly.

"Gracias," Vicky said in a defeated tone and she walked on. She followed the bend in the road, her steps dragging. This is pointless, she thought. Even if Ben

had come this far on his own, how could she ever hope to find him in this confusing network of streets and houses.

Just then, Vicky heard a child's high-pitched shriek, followed by a splash. Her heart stopped. Could that be Ben? The sound had come from the house on her left. She flew up the driveway and through the gate.

Matt lay prone at the edge of the pool, his arms thrust into the water. He gave her a startled glance. Vicky ran forward and saw the small figure thrashing wildly in the pool. Matt's left hand grasped Ben's arm above the elbow and with his right hand he took a firmer grip on the back of the boy's shorts. Grunting with effort, Matt pulled Ben to the surface. Vicky dropped to her knees beside him and grabbed Ben's other arm. Together they dragged him out of the pool. She clutched her son to her. He was coughing and choking. Vicky bent him over her arm and thumped him on the back. Then, her face streaming with tears, she sobbed, "Oh God!" and crushed Ben against her breast.

For a moment, no one spoke. Finally, still coughing a bit, Ben said, "Mommy?"

"Yes, sweetheart?"

"Mommy, the man said some other kids were coming to play, but they never did."

"We'll talk about it later, honey. Let's get home." Vicky stood up, still holding Ben tight. The three of them walked out of the gate and down the drive.

As they trudged slowly down the hill, Vicky said to Matt, "Thank God you were there. What happened?"

"I'd gone as far as the end of the road, and I was on my way back when I thought I heard the sound of a bouncing ball coming from behind that house. The

place looked closed up; it made me wonder. I
to the back and opened the gate. Ben was standing at
the edge of the pool. I guess I must have startled him.
He seemed to lose his balance and he fell into the
water. You came along just as I got to him," Matt
explained.

Vicky shook her head. "I can't believe it. What
would have happened if you hadn't found him?"

Matt smiled at her reassuringly. "At least
everything's okay now."

By the time they had turned onto Seaview, Ben had
demanded to be put down. His eyes widened. "Mom!
There's police cars by *our* house!"

"Yes," she explained, "the police were looking for
you. We didn't know where you were. We thought you
were lost."

Puzzled, Ben looked up at his mother. "I was at that
man's house."

Officer Robinson stood by his squad car, talking
into the microphone. When he spotted Vicky, Ben, and
Matt coming toward him, he said a few more words,
then went to meet them.

"Hello there, young man. So you're the one who's
been causing all the commotion." He bent down to
Ben's eye level.

"What's 'commotion'?" asked Ben.

"We were pretty worried about you," the officer
continued kindly. "I'd like to hear all about where you
went. Let's go in the house." He stuck out his large
hand, and Ben took it trustingly. The tall black
policeman and the little carrot-topped boy walked
together up the front steps.

Mrs. Garfield saw them coming and yanked open
the front door. "Oh, Ben, thank the Lord!" she cried as

...own and hugged him. "Wherever have ...Ben could answer, the policeman broke in. ...think we'll all sit down and relax, and let Ben ...his story." He herded them into the living room ...perched Ben on a chair. The boy was enjoying the attention, and eagerly watched the officer squat down in front of him.

"Okay, Ben. Can you tell us what you did after you got off the school bus this afternoon?"

"Sure," said Ben. He told them about the man who had taken him to play at the pool. When asked, he described the man as well as he could, but when it was over, Ben had been able to give the policeman no useful information.

Officer Robinson drew Matt aside to find out what he could add to the story. Then he turned to Vicky. "Mr. London's going to take us to the house and we'll check it out, Mrs. Hunter. But it sounds as if whoever did this knew what he was doing. I'm pretty sure it will turn out that the people who own it are out of town and had nothing at all to do with it."

"Well, what are you going to *do*?" asked Vicky, her voice beginning to rise.

"Now, ma'am, the boy's fine. He's not even scared," he said peaceably. "And there's nothing we *can* do. It could have been some sort of crazy prank. Anyway, we have nothing to go on."

"You mean you're just going to leave and forget about it?"

"Mrs. Hunter, your getting upset will only frighten your boy. Just keep an eye on him. And call us if you have any more problems. Of any kind." He tousled Ben's hair and gave him a grin. "'Bye, Ben."

she swooped down and hugged him. "Wherever have you been?"

Before Ben could answer, the policeman broke in. "Now, I think we'll all sit down and relax, and let Ben tell us his story." He herded them into the living room and perched Ben on a chair. The boy was enjoying the attention, and eagerly watched the officer squat down in front of him.

"Okay, Ben. Can you tell us what you did after you got off the school bus this afternoon?"

"Sure," said Ben. He told them about the man who had taken him to play at the pool. When asked, he described the man as well as he could, but when it was over, Ben had been able to give the policeman no useful information.

Officer Robinson drew Matt aside to find out what he could add to the story. Then he turned to Vicky. "Mr. London's going to take us to the house and we'll check it out, Mrs. Hunter. But it sounds as if whoever did this knew what he was doing. I'm pretty sure it will turn out that the people who own it are out of town and had nothing at all to do with it."

"Well, what are you going to *do*?" asked Vicky, her voice beginning to rise.

"Now, ma'am, the boy's fine. He's not even scared," he said peaceably. "And there's nothing we *can* do. It could have been some sort of crazy prank. Anyway, we have nothing to go on."

"You mean you're just going to leave and forget about it?"

"Mrs. Hunter, your getting upset will only frighten your boy. Just keep an eye on him. And call us if you have any more problems. Of any kind." He tousled Ben's hair and gave him a grin. "'Bye, Ben."

place looked closed up; it made me wonder. I went to the back and opened the gate. Ben was standing at the edge of the pool. I guess I must have startled him. He seemed to lose his balance and he fell into the water. You came along just as I got to him," Matt explained.

Vicky shook her head. "I can't believe it. What would have happened if you hadn't found him?"

Matt smiled at her reassuringly. "At least everything's okay now."

By the time they had turned onto Seaview, Ben had demanded to be put down. His eyes widened. "Mom! There's police cars by *our* house!"

"Yes," she explained, "the police were looking for you. We didn't know where you were. We thought you were lost."

Puzzled, Ben looked up at his mother. "I was at that man's house."

Officer Robinson stood by his squad car, talking into the microphone. When he spotted Vicky, Ben, and Matt coming toward him, he said a few more words, then went to meet them.

"Hello there, young man. So you're the one who's been causing all the commotion." He bent down to Ben's eye level.

"What's 'commotion'?" asked Ben.

"We were pretty worried about you," the officer continued kindly. "I'd like to hear all about where you went. Let's go in the house." He stuck out his large hand, and Ben took it trustingly. The tall black policeman and the little carrot-topped boy walked together up the front steps.

Mrs. Garfield saw them coming and yanked open the front door. "Oh, Ben, thank the Lord!" she cried as

As Matt left with the policeman, he gave Vicky an encouraging smile. "I shouldn't be too long. While I'm gone, why don't you decide where you and Ben would like to go for dinner."

"McDonald's!" Ben shouted without a moment's hesitation.

Matt shot a questioning look at Vicky, and seeing that she had no objections, said, "You got it, Ben. See you in a little while."

Vicky turned to Mrs. Garfield as the men went out the door. "I can't thank you enough," she began.

"Well, I'm just glad it all turned out all right. I surely am happy to see Ben safe and sound." She picked up her knitting. "I'll be leaving—I can see you've got everything under control. But if there's anything I can do—anything at all—just give me a holler."

As she left, Vicky said to Ben, "I think I'll pop you into the tub. Then you can wear your new green jeans out to dinner."

"Mom," Ben said slowly. "I didn't go in the pool on purpose."

Vicky wrapped her arms around him, her eyes stinging with tears. "I know you didn't, sweetheart. And we're not going to talk about it anymore."

Chapter 4

Ben's Big Mac dripped all over the table as he took another bite. Vicky gave him a smile. Dinner at McDonald's was a special occasion for him, and he was obviously suffering no ill effects from his experience that afternoon. He doesn't realize there was anything to be scared of, she thought. She was glad he wasn't frightened, but she wished there were some way to make him more cautious. On the other hand, she hated to spoil his innocent enthusiasm for life—she certainly didn't want to turn him into one of those kids who were afraid of anything new.

She toyed with the styrofoam coffee cup. Still too keyed-up and tense, she hadn't been able to face eating anything. Matt and Ben were deep in a discussion about police cars. Ben had been thrilled at the chance to sit in a real squad car and look at all the dials and switches. Officer Robinson had even let Ben turn on the flashing red light when he'd brought Matt back to the house. Vicky could just hear the exciting tales Ben would tell at school the next day.

When Ben had finished his last french fry, they stood up and went out to the parking lot. As they drove home, Matt kept Ben talking about cars and radios, sensing that Vicky hadn't yet shaken off her reaction to the terrifying incident.

"Jerry's dad has a radio in his car," Ben remarked.

"You mean a CB radio?" Matt asked, pulling into Vicky's driveway.

"The kind you talk to. Why don't you have one?" he went on, jumping down as Matt held the door open for him. "Then you could talk to people."

"Well, I don't really—" Matt began.

Vicky roused herself. "Not everybody wants to talk while they're driving, honey. Now let's go inside; it's almost bedtime."

As she fished for her front door key, Matt spoke from behind her. "You must be exhausted. You've had a long day. I guess I ought to push off."

"Oh no," Vicky said quickly, "not unless you want to. Why don't you come in for a while? I'm just going to get Ben into bed."

The three of them trooped inside. "Say good night to Matt, Ben."

He obediently echoed, "Good night," and Vicky said, "Help yourself to a drink, Matt. I won't be long."

She got Ben into his pajamas and read him a story, holding him on her lap and feeling that she could hardly bear to let go of him. Hugging him fiercely, she put him into bed.

As if in response to her unspoken thoughts, Ben

looked up. "I love you, Mommy."

Bending to kiss him again, she said softly, "I love you too, Ben. Good night."

She closed the door gently, and walked down the hallway to the living room. Matt looked up as she sank onto the couch. Kicking off her shoes, she tucked her feet under her. Matt handed her a glass.

"I thought you could use a drink; hope this is okay."

"Thanks," she said. "I feel as though I can hardly move."

"I'll bet," he said, giving her a sympathetic look. "You didn't eat anything; you must be wiped out."

"I was too knotted up inside. I couldn't even look at that food. It feels good to sit down and unwind."

Matt stood up. "You just stay where you are and take it easy. I'm going to make you some soup. You really should have something to eat."

"Oh, you don't have to do that," Vicky protested.

He held up a hand to silence her. "Leave it to me. I may look like a klutz, but I do know how to operate a can opener." He grinned and went out to the kitchen.

Vicky tucked a pillow behind her head and leaned back. I'm glad Matt is here, she thought wearily. What would I have done if he hadn't shown up? Fragments of the afternoon chased one another through her mind: her first phone call to Mrs. Garfield; the arrival of the police at her door; her encounter with the kids in the playground; helping Matt pull Ben from the pool. She heard again the questions Officer Rosales had asked while Matt guided Robinson to the empty house.

"Who is this Matt London that found your son?"

Vicky had explained that Matt was an old friend of her husband's. She herself had only known him a few days, but he'd been very kind and had taken a great deal of interest in Ben. She had caught the policewoman's speculative look.

"How did he happen to be here this afternoon? Were you expecting him?"

"He was going to come for dinner. He must have decided to come over early and play with Ben or something. Anyway, it's a good thing he did."

Officer Rosales had nodded noncommittally. "I see. Now could you tell me again exactly what Mr. London said happened before you arrived at the pool?"

Patiently, Vicky had gone through it all again. It sounds as if the police don't believe Matt's story! she thought indignantly.

She reflected now that it wasn't their fault. Police were trained to be suspicious of everything, and they probably thought they had to ask all kinds of questions. After all, they had no way of knowing what kind of person Matt was.

But the question still remained—who had taken Ben to that house? She didn't have much hope that the police would find out anything useful. Vicky shivered. Who could it have been?

"I know it wasn't an accident," she said aloud, just as Matt returned carrying a tray.

He set the tray down carefully. "Well, I managed not to spill it," he said with a laugh. "Now, forget about what's happened for a while, and eat this while it's hot."

She smiled back at him. "It looks good—and you even made toast! What a treat to be waited on." She picked up the bowl of soup.

"Oh, I'm a whiz in the kitchen. You'll be happy to know that I only used fourteen saucepans and every knife and spoon I could find."

Vicky appreciated his efforts to cheer her up, and she wished she could respond. She swallowed several spoonfuls of the warm soup in silence. Finally she said, "I'm sorry, I'm not very good company tonight. I can't stop thinking about what's going on. It's hard to deal with the idea that someone is trying to hurt me and Ben."

"Well..." Matt began, but Vicky continued on.

"It can't all be coincidence—too much has happened. First the phone calls, then someone forces me off the road, and now this thing today. And I'm beginning to think that someone purposely opened the gate and hoped Ben would go into the street and get run over."

"Come on now, Vicky."

"No, I'm serious."

"But you're making it sound like there's a bunch of gangsters after you. How could you be mixed up with people like that? You're not a secret spy for the Mafia, are you?"

Ignoring his attempt at humor, Vicky said seriously, "That's just it. I can't imagine why anyone wants to hurt us. And the worst part of it is that it always seems to involve Ben, too."

Matt nodded. "I guess I can understand how you feel. It must be hard to have that kind of responsibility. Especially when you're the only parent Ben has. He probably can hardly remember Tom."

"Oh, he knows who his father was. I've tried very hard to tell him about Tom and let him know he had a daddy. We look at the photo I have in my room, and he asks me all kinds of questions."

"I think that's very important for Ben," Matt said.

"And I think it will mean even more to him when

he's older," Vicky continued. "I've already given him one of Tom's old baseballs. There's a whole lot of that stuff out in the garage. And there's a huge envelope of papers in the bottom drawer of the desk. I'm not even sure what's in it—it might just be old term papers from college or something. I haven't been able to make myself go through it yet. But when I do, I'm sure there will be a lot of things that I'll want to save for Ben."

"Yes," Matt said slowly, "I can see that having a child is a major responsibility. Maybe that's what Suzanne meant."

"Suzanne?"

"My ex-wife never wanted to have any children—that was one of our problems. She always said she didn't want the responsibility of a child."

"Hmmm," Vicky said. "That's too bad."

"That's what I thought. It seemed to me that the good parts of it would far outweigh the difficulties. But she didn't look at it that way. I'm not sure she thought there would be any good parts. She seemed to feel it would be nothing but drudgery—a burden."

He paused, reliving his painful memories. Then he shook his head. "I guess it's a good thing we didn't have any kids. But I always thought it would be great to watch a kid grow up and help him discover the world. I don't think I would have minded the problems." He looked at Vicky. "I bet Tom was thrilled to have a baby—he must have been a real proud papa. Ben is such a super kid."

"Thanks, I think so myself," Vicky said with a little laugh.

"Okay," said Matt, picking up the tray. "Now you'll get to sample my fabulous coffee."

Vicky watched him disappear again into the

kitchen. Poor Matt—he obviously wanted to have a family. And he seemed to grasp the ups and downs of raising children. Tom certainly had enjoyed the ups. He'd loved playing with Ben and showing him off to their friends. He'd even helped with the feeding and bathing and diapering. But then the terrible memories came flooding back of how Tom had collapsed when their son had been so sick. Ben was only six months old, when she went in to check on him one night. He felt awfully hot, and she called to Tom to get the thermometer. When Ben whimpered as she took his temperature, Tom seemed to lose control. He tried to pull her hand away, saying, "You're hurting him!" She sent him to call the doctor, but on the phone he became completely incoherent. She picked Ben up and went to talk to the doctor herself. Ben's temperature was over a hundred and four, and the doctor said he'd meet them in the emergency room. She hung up to find Tom sobbing uncontrollably on the couch. Without lifting his head, he said brokenly, "He's got brain damage— my boy. He'll never be able to do anything." Vicky tried to reason with him, but in the end, she had to bundle Ben up and drive him to the hospital herself. It turned out to be roseola—scary but not serious. She listened to the doctor's instructions and then took Ben home. She and the baby had a rough couple of days, with lukewarm baths, temperature-taking, and careful doses of baby aspirin every few hours. By the third day, the spots appeared and Ben was fine. That night, Tom came home with red roses for both of them—but she felt she could never count on him again.

Matt reappeared, triumphantly bearing two steaming mugs of coffee. He glanced at Vicky's sad and withdrawn expression. She seemed sunk in thought.

"Now, Vicky," he chided her with mock severity, "I haven't been working myself to a frazzle in the kitchen just so you could sit out here and dwell on the whole business of this afternoon." He set down the coffee cups.

His voice brought her out of her reverie. She felt vaguely disloyal. This was the first time she'd thought of that incident since Tom's death.

"I know it was upsetting, but it's all over now. It's not going to happen again," Matt went on.

Vicky looked up at him. "Sorry. You've been great to take care of me like this."

"Everyone needs a little TLC now and then." He sipped at his coffee. "I know you're tired. Whenever you want me to leave, just say the word."

"I was just thinking of how glad I was that you came in after dinner. It sounds stupid, but I was nervous about coming in by myself. I guess I imagined someone lurking in the shadows."

"Look" said Matt easily, "my van's right outside. I can sleep out there in the driveway if it will make you feel any safer."

"Oh, Matt," said Vicky, "I *would* feel safer. But it's crazy for you to stay out there. You can sleep in here on the couch."

"Fine," said Matt. He realized that Vicky was practically asleep on her feet. "You look like you could do with a good night's sleep."

"I am a little tired," she admitted. Then she jumped up. "I'll just pull out some sheets and blankets. It won't take me a minute."

"Can't I help?" he asked. But Vicky waved away his offer.

"No. I'm one of those people who puts everything in

its place and then can't remember where the place is. I'll do better on my own." She walked out of the living room, muttering to herself, "Let's see, I think the pillows are in my closet, behind..."

Sure enough, Vicky returned a few minutes later, her arms piled high with bedding. She and Matt made up the couch together. "Well, good night, Matt," Vicky said as soon as they'd finished.

"Good night, Vicky." He put a hand on her shoulder and squeezed gently. "And don't worry, I'll be right here all night. Sleep well."

As Vicky padded down the hall, she felt the lingering warmth of his strong grasp. Washing her face in the bathroom, she heard the front door open and close. Matt was going out to get his toothbrush from the van. It was nice of him to change his plans and stay overnight in the house. Vicky left the night light on in the bathroom and crawled into bed. Now she felt that she could get some sleep. She felt safe.

Matt sat on the couch and read as the lights went out in Vicky's room and the house grew quiet. For a long time he didn't move, waiting until he was sure Vicky was fast asleep. Then, stealthily, he got up and walked with silent footsteps to the desk. He switched on the little desk lamp and pulled open the bottom drawer. The fat envelope was jammed in all the way at the back, just as Vicky had said. Carefully, he extracted it. It was a large manila envelope, kept together with rubber bands and bulging at the seams. Matt laid the envelope on the desk. After removing the rubber bands, he took out all the papers and started going through them. It was tedious work. Even when he found what he was looking for, he had to search the rest of the stack to be sure there was nothing else he needed. Then, listening for any noises in the house, he refilled the envelope and returned it to the drawer. He stopped to listen again. Nothing. Quickly, Matt folded the two sheets of paper he had kept out. He switched off the lamp and carried them back to the couch. As soon as he'd concealed them in his jacket pocket, he sighed with relief. Then he rolled his jacket up and shoved it under his pillow. In moments he was asleep.

Chapter 5

It was ten after eight on Saturday morning, and Matt's van was heading south on the San Diego Freeway. Matt glanced over at Vicky and smiled.

"This was a great idea of yours. I've always wanted to go to Mexico."

Vicky laughed. "Rosarito Beach isn't exactly the heart of Old Mexico. But once we get past Tijuana, at least it won't be just a trap for tourists."

"Mom," Ben piped up, "can I play with my pail and shovel when we get to Rosie Beach?"

"Sure, honey. We'll go down to the beach this afternoon. Maybe we'll find some shells there." She turned to Matt. "I hope this place hasn't changed too much. I wouldn't want your first look at Mexico to be a disappointment."

"Oh, it won't be. And the hotel you've been talking about sounds terrific."

"Yes, it really was a wonderful place to stay—elegance gone to seed, right out of a movie set. But don't forget, I haven't been there for almost five years. I hope the seedy part hasn't entirely taken over."

"Don't worry," Matt reassured her. "If it's too grubby, we'll find someplace else—or we can always sleep in the van."

Vicky laughed. "Yes, you're certainly well prepared. Even this front seat would make an extra bed in an emergency."

"I guess so," Matt replied. "The guy I bought the van from had a little girl who liked to ride up front, so he put in a bench seat instead of the buckets. The middle section is a little short on leg room, but I guess Ben doesn't mind." He smiled at the boy beside him.

Vicky looked out the window and gave a little sigh of contentment. "I'm glad we decided to do this. I needed to get away for a couple of days."

He smiled at her again as the van rolled southward. On both sides of the freeway as far as they could see were solidly built-up expanses of streets and small houses. Each community merged into the next without a break. Nearing Long Beach, houses gave way to vast areas of industrial plants.

"Ugh!" Matt exclaimed. "What's that revolting smell?"

As Ben held his nose, Vicky waved in the direction of the huge, round, monolithic structures that squatted to their right. The effect was of a futuristic wasteland.

"I have no idea what it is, but that smell is always here. It's awful, isn't it?"

The freeway carried them into Orange County, with its welter of tightly packed developments. Finally the dry, rolling hills of the Irvine Ranch came into view.

Hawks wheeled overhead, and the long brown grass riffled in the wind.

"I've always liked this stretch of country," Vicky said. "Too bad it's starting to get built up. Pretty soon we'll have a solid corridor of pavement and tract houses from L.A. to the border."

Before long, they could smell the ocean again. A green-and-white freeway sign said: Next Exit—San Juan Capistrano.

"Look at that! I didn't know that was a real place," Matt commented.

"Oh yes," said Vicky, "and the swallows really do come back every spring. Maybe we'll come down here one day—it's a lovely little mission church."

"What did they swallow, Mom?" Ben asked.

Both Matt and Vicky chuckled. "Swallows are a kind of bird," she explained. "Every winter they fly away, and then, on a certain day in spring, they fly back to that town we just passed."

"Why?" asked Ben.

"Well..." Vicky paused. "The birds go farther south where it's warmer for the winter."

"Why?" Ben persisted. He could ask that question almost indefinitely. Vicky tried not to get suckered into these frustrating conversations, but now and then he caught her off guard.

As they sped down a gentle grade, the sparkling Pacific came into view. "Oh, look! The ocean!" said Vicky, hoping to distract Ben. It worked.

"Is that the same ocean as ours?" he asked.

"Yes, Ben, it is," Vicky replied.

As they neared San Diego, Matt looked at his watch. "We've made pretty good time so far. Do I stay on this highway or what?"

"Watch for 805. I think it drops straight down to the border now. I'll let you know when to stop for insurance."

"Insurance? What for?"

"Oh, I forgot, you probably don't know about getting Mexican car insurance. Anybody who drives across the border is crazy if he doesn't get some." Matt glanced at her in surprise, and Vicky went on, "In Mexico, if you're involved in any sort of car accident, whether it's your fault or not, the cops can throw you in jail till it's all sorted out. If you've got a Mex-Insur sticker on your windshield, they'll usually let you go without any big hassle."

"Nice racket," Matt commented.

"Well, I've never seen the inside of a Mexican jail, but they're not billed as the best."

The giant green-and-white freeway sign stretching across the road over their heads warned: U.S.-Mexico Border 1000 Yards Ahead. After a brief stop at the Mex-Insur office, the van slowed at the border. Across the road was something that looked like a string of covered toll booths. At each drive-through, a bored-looking, dark-eyed man in uniform glanced at the cars as they passed. The border guard smiled at Matt and Vicky, and waved to Ben as Matt drove by. Up ahead a sign said: Tijuana 1 Mile.

Matt looked at Vicky in surprise. "That's it?"

"That's it. We're across. Welcome to Mexico," laughed Vicky.

The signs were confusing, but eventually they found a road they hoped would skirt around the edge of Tijuana and head down to Rosarito. The dirt-covered blacktop twisted back north, and suddenly they found themselves riding right beside the border fence. Tall and sturdy-looking chain link was topped by numerous strands of barbed wire. On the U.S. side, farm fields stretched north. The three of them eyed the fence with interest.

"Why is that jacket on the fence?" Ben asked. Flapping in the breeze, a man's jacket was caught securely by one sleeve about halfway up.

"I don't know, honey," said Vicky.

A few yards farther along, a patterned shirt that looked as if it had been there for some time was tangled in the barbed wire. As they drove along, more articles of clothing were caught here and there on the fence, and a battered cardboard suitcase lay abandoned on the Mexico side. Vicky and Matt exchanged a glance. These pathetic remnants were poignant reminders that the U.S. represented the only hope for many of Mexico's poor citizens.

On the other side of the road, washing hung dispiritedly on clotheslines outside tarpaper shacks. Rutted dirt paths wound crazily among the buildings, and a few chickens scratched in the dust. Dark-eyed children stared at the van as it passed. Vicky was uncomfortably aware of the contrast between these barefooted tots in their ragged clothes and her own sturdy, bright-faced son.

Vicky shook off her depression. Now they were traveling beside the scruffy hills of the Baja; the ocean glinted up at them on their right. She knew they were nearing Rosarito when the houses with yards full of gaily painted pots came into view.

"Not far now," Vicky said. "Keep your eyes open for the archway—it says Rosarito Beach Hotel."

Soon they were turning into the courtyard of the rambling old hotel. As they walked into the cavernous lobby, Matt stopped and looked around.

"It's fabulous, Vicky! I feel as though Pancho Villa may appear any minute."

"I'm glad you like it—it's just the way I remembered."

The desk clerk was too polite to do more than raise an inquiring eyebrow when Matt asked for two separate rooms. They arranged for a cot to be set up in Vicky's room for Ben, and then went up the wide, curving staircase.

When they met again, dressed for the beach, Vicky led the way across the enormous dining room and through the glass doors to the pool.

"I hope we can get some lunch out here. Wait till you see the inside of this bar."

The building by the pool was furnished entirely in turn-of-the-century rattan. Windows overlooked the pool and the beach below. The smiling bartender came over to their table. "*Sí, señor, señora?* What is it that you wish?"

Vicky tried out her Spanish. "*Es posible para comer aquí?*"

His smile widened and he bowed slightly. It was always a pleasant surprise when a tourist spoke even a little Spanish. Most of them acted as though Mexico was just an appendage of *los Estados Unidos grandes.* "*Sí, señora, para usted.*"

After a short consultation, Vicky ordered tostadas and enchiladas for herself and Matt, and a toasted cheese sandwich for Ben. While they ate, Ben bobbed up and down in his chair, looking out the window. He was amazed to see people on horseback, riding up and down at the water's edge, and could hardly wait for a closer look at them.

Ben raced ahead as, after lunch, they walked down the steps to the sand. The horses had disappeared, but there were several children digging a huge hole. Ben ran over and stood watching. One of the boys looked up and smiled, and Ben immediately jumped down to join in the project.

Vicky and Matt sat down on the warm sand.

"Ah, this is the life!" Matt sighed with satisfaction.

"Mmm," Vicky agreed. "Actually, it seems kind of silly to come all the way down here and sit on the beach, when I have a perfectly good beach a couple of blocks from my house. But it's nice to get away. I feel more relaxed already." She tilted her head back, and the two of them soaked up the sun.

"Maria, Manuel! Vengas aquí. Vamonos." A pleasant-looking young Mexican woman came down from the hotel and called to the children with whom Ben was playing. By now, only the tops of their heads were visible. Sand was flying up over the edge of the enormous hole. As the eager diggers kept working, a girl's voice floated up.

"Sí, sí, Mama, un momento."

The woman stood near the edge of the hole, her hands on her hips. She shook her head resignedly. *"Un momento—siempre un momento."*

Vicky got to her feet and bent to brush the sand from the backs of her legs. She ambled over and peered into the excavation site.

"Having fun, Ben?" He nodded without glancing up from his shovel. "Looks like you kids are halfway to China already." She looked at the other mother and smiled. *"Mi niño le gusta este."*

The young woman laughed. "My children also. They do not wish to leave when I call for them."

The two of them stood watching the children, chatting in a mixture of Spanish and English. The woman and her husband were also staying at the hotel. They were from Mexicali and had brought the children for a week at the seashore.

Finally she called her children again, and this time she wasn't taking no for an answer. Vicky helped her pull the children up onto the dry sand. The boy and girl turned and waved. "*Adios*, Ben!"

"They like your boy. Not often do they see this red hair," explained their mother.

Vicky and Ben watched them as they made their way toward the hotel. On the steps, a heavyset Mexican man in a brightly patterned shirt sat watching them. Vicky thought, that must be her husband—he looks a lot older than she is. But the woman and her kids walked past him without speaking.

Vicky turned to Matt. "How about walking up the beach a ways?"

They strolled along the water's edge, their feet squelching in the wet sand. Ben circled around them, darting in and out of the waves and splashing happily. He collected shells and bits of kelp, storing these treasures in his sand pail, which Vicky was carrying.

Matt bent down and scooped something from a retreating wave. "Look, Ben, a sand dollar."

Vicky and Ben examined the object in his outstretched hand. "What a good one," Vicky exclaimed. "It's not even chipped around the edge."

She helped Ben put it carefully in the bottom of the pail. "Let's see if we can find any more."

They walked on a bit farther, and then turned back

the way they had come. Coming toward them was the heavyset man, his black shirt with printed red palm trees sticking to his arms and chest. He was wearing street shoes with pointy toes, and kept to the dry sand farther in from the water.

"Must be hot," Matt commented. "He's not exactly dressed for the beach."

"No," Vicky agreed. "I saw him sitting on the hotel steps a while ago."

As they passed, the man raised his eyes briefly. A few minutes later, he paused and turned to watch their retreating figures.

"Do you think Ben's legs can handle a little more walking?" Matt asked. "I'd like to explore the town."

"Oh, sure. Sounds like fun."

Rosarito Beach had grown up along the major highway that ran south from the border through Baja California. The closest town to Tijuana along the coast, it had been a thriving tourist resort in the prewar years. But the new toll road bypassed Rosarito to the east and made it easier to reach the beach towns farther down the peninsula. Several enclaves of beach houses for rich Americans had sprung up over the years, just to the south of the town, each one bringing a brief surge of vitality to the community. But most of these seemed to wither away, and Rosarito relapsed into somnolence, almost untouched by the changes of the past several decades.

Small, dusty streets branched off the old highway bisecting the town. Open-fronted *tiendas* offered tourist wares—leather sandals, local pottery, silver jewelry from Taxco, a wide variety of colorful ethnic clothing—as well as goods for the townspeople. The spicy scent of jalapeno peppers and hot frying fat hung in the air, and vendors sold fruit ices and hot, cinnamon-scented *bolillos*. Underfoot, scrawny dogs ran among the children playing in the streets.

Vicky kept a tight hold on Ben's hand as the three of them wandered through the bustling marketplace, admiring the black earthenware from Oaxaca. Matt stopped to look at a rack of embroidered shirts.

"*Sí, señor?* You like to buy? Very good prices." The shopkeeper materialized at Matt's elbow.

"Can I try it on? I don't know if it's big enough."

"Sure, ees okay." He pulled two shirts from the other side of the rack and held them out. "These good for you—you very big man."

Matt pulled the shirt over his head. "How do I look?" he asked Vicky. "Do you like it?"

"Looks great," she answered.

"Well, it may be corny, but I need a souvenir. How much?" he asked the shopkeeper.

"That one, *señor*, two hundred and sixty pesos."

"Hmm," Matt said. He walked farther into the shop and peered around. "Do you have a shirt for the boy?" he asked, indicating Ben.

"Sure, yes, I have." He opened a drawer and took out a pile of small shirts with colorful embroidery.

"Come on and tell me which one you like, Ben," Matt said. Together they chose one with stripes of variegated color at neck and wrists, and Ben tried it on. He looked suddenly grown up and very charming.

"How much?" asked Matt again.

"*Por dos*, for both, *señor*, three hundred and sixty pesos."

Matt shook his head regretfully. "Well, I don't think I can..."

"Okay, you take both, three hundred and twenty-five."

Matt looked doubtful. "I don't know." He looked carefully at the embroidery on one sleeve, and then began to pull off the shirt. The shopkeeper took hold of the hem and pulled the shirt back down.

"Very good quality, *señor*. All handmade. You don't find this in other stores. All these shirts made by hand." He waved a hand at Ben. "Nice shirt for the boy. Many colors." He adjusted Ben's shirt to show how well it fit.

Matt didn't say anything. At last the shopkeeper said, "You give me three hundred pesos—okay?"

Looking at Vicky, Matt said, "What do you think?"

"Well, it's a lot of money," she said slowly.

The shopkeeper threw his hands up. "Okay, okay. Two hundred eighty pesos, no cheaper."

"All right," said Matt. "Two hundred eighty." He counted out the money while the shopkeeper continued to extol the merits of the shirts. At last he smiled and said, *"Gracias, señor, señora. Adios."*

As they emerged into the street, Vicky said, "Wow. Who would have guessed you were such a shrewd bargainer?"

Matt smiled. "Us north woods folk have a lot of native cunning. But what about you? We've got to find something for you. What would you like?"

She began to protest, but he persisted. Finally she said, "The only thing I really want is a couple of pots for the front of the house. Let's look for some tomorrow outside the town."

They sauntered slowly back to the hotel, successfully dissuading Ben from sampling the food vendors' greasy delicacies. When they reached the hotel, they went upstairs to wash off the dust before dinner.

An hour later, they met in the dining room. Ben was scrubbed and shiny, and he had refused to consider wearing anything but his new shirt. Several heads turned to watch his colorful figure as he marched between the tables, and Maria and Manuel waved from the other side of the room.

The hotel might be old, but the food and service were still superb. Vicky and Matt finished their *ceviche*, that tasty blend of marinated raw fish and onion, while Ben munched on one of the delicious hard rolls.

Then the entrees arrived—steaming shrimp and rice for Ben and beautiful red snapper grilled with lemon and cilantro for the two adults.

As they ate, they could see the moon outside the window. Nearly full, it was so bright that the water glittered and sparkled as far as they could see.

"Looks like a perfect evening for a walk on the beach," Matt said. "Maybe we could go out for a stroll and a drink after Ben goes to bed."

"Oh, I'd love to." She paused. "But I can't leave Ben alone in the room—he'd be pretty scared if he woke up."

"Oh. Okay," Matt said in disappointment.

The waiter came to take away their empty plates, and they ordered creme caramel, the restaurant's specialty, for dessert. Vicky saw Manuel and Maria, trailed by their parents, approaching from across the room.

"Good evening," said the woman. "The children wish to say good night to your son."

Matt stood up and they all introduced themselves.

As the men shook hands, Vicky said with sudden inspiration to Señora Alvarez, "Do you know how I can find a babysitter to stay with my son this evening?" Seeing the woman's puzzled look, she added, *"Una señorita por el niño, esta noche?"*

"Oh, *sí*." Senora Alvarez's face brightened. "Ask for the manager of the hotel. He will find a nice girl." She waved a hand. "Maybe from the kitchen."

"Oh, good," Vicky said. "This girl will stay in the room?"

"Yes, the girls like the children, do not worry." She grinned and collected her children. *"Buenas noches,* Ben."

Señor Alvarez gave them a formal smile as they turned to leave.

After dessert, Vicky led the way to the front desk. The manager, polite and helpful, assured them that a trustworthy *señorita* would be at Vicky's door promptly at eight. Vicky was happily surprised at the low wages he suggested.

"I will send a boy to put up a screen *momentito*." He went on in explanation, "The light will not keep the *niño* awake."

Sure enough, the screen was in the room when Vicky and Ben went upstairs. Promptly at eight, there was a knock on the door. Vicky opened it for a shy-looking girl of about eighteen. She said her name was Rosa. In the plastic bag under her arm she had two or three movie magazines and the beginnings of a string-crochet bedspread.

Vicky introduced her to Ben and asked Rosa if she could speak any English. Rose hung her head. *"No, señora,"* she replied softly.

"Okay." Vicky turned to Ben. "Rosa is going to stay

with you while Matt and I are downstairs for a while. So you jump into bed and I'll tuck you in. Rosa will be here if you need anything."

"But I'm not sleepy," Ben protested.

"Well, it's bedtime anyway, so you hop in and maybe Rosa can sing you a little song." She pulled up the covers and gave him a kiss. "I'll see you in the morning, sweetie."

Vicky picked up her shawl and told Rosa she would be back no later than eleven. *"El niño dice que no le gusta a dormir, pero pienso el duerme en pocos minutos."*

Rosa smiled understandingly. *"Sí, señora."*

"Es posible para canta usted por el?"

Vicky wasn't sure she had gotten her message across, but Rosa replied quickly, *"Sí, sí, señora, entiendo. No es una problema."*

She pulled the chair over next to Ben's cot and sat down, her crocheting in her lap. As Vicky left, she could hear Rosa's voice murmuring gently to Ben.

Matt and Vicky walked slowly down the beach. The giant hole the children had dug gaped darkly up at them. "Wonder if those canal-builders knew what kind of cheap labor they were passing up?" Matt said with a grin. Vicky's laugh was carried away by the cool ocean breeze. Matt looked at her appraisingly.

"It's good to hear you sound so happy and carefree."

"I guess I left all my worries in L.A."

"That must mean that I'm a good influence on you," Matt said lightly.

Thoughtfully, Vicky said, "It's funny. I feel as though I've known you all my life, but I really don't know much about you at all."

"What do you mean?"

"Well, like I don't have a clue about what kind of book you're writing."

"It's supposed to be a novel," Matt said easily. "Sort of about the advertising business."

"An exposé?"

"Not exactly," he answered with a laugh. "I'm really not far enough along yet to know what it's going to be."

"Well, then. Tell me about yourself—where you grew up and all."

Matt laughed. "You want the whole story or the condensed version?"

"Just start when you were born," she said gaily.

Matt told her a little about his childhood in Canfield, Ohio. "My mom and dad still live in the same house, and Dad still works in the hardware store."

"Where's your sister?"

"Oh, she got married to her high-school sweetheart, and they live about ten miles from Mom and Dad. I haven't been back to see any of them for quite a while."

"So then what happened?" asked Vicky.

"Well, I got a football scholarship to Washington State. Luckily my grades held up, because I discovered I didn't much like getting my brains battered in by the big guys. I finished up on a government loan and a string of jobs hashing at the frat houses."

"That must be how you met Tom," Vicky guessed. "He told me about those crummy jobs he had when he was working his way through school."

Matt looked at her in surprise, but before he could say anything, she went on, "What happened after college? How did you end up in Portland?"

"Oh, you know how it goes. One thing led to another."

It was clear that Matt didn't want to disclose that

phase of his life. I wonder if that was a difficult time for him, Vicky mused. Well, if he wanted to keep it to himself, she wouldn't push him.

They continued along the deserted beach in silence. Without competing city lights, the stars were bright in the vast sky above. When they reached a stone breakwater crossing the sand, Matt took Vicky's hand and helped her climb up and over it. Hand in hand, they fled, chased by the changing tide that threatened to wash over their sandals. Reaching the high-tide line, they stopped, laughing breathlessly.

"Looks like we'll have to go back by the road," Vicky said.

"I think you're right," Matt agreed. Then he drew her to him. His strong arms went around her, and he bent his face toward hers. As their lips met, Vicky's hands slid up his chest to his shoulders, and she felt the warmth of his strong body against her.

A moment later, she stiffened and pushed away, averting her face. Matt raised his head and gazed out over her dark hair.

"You're still in love with him, aren't you?"

"I guess I am," Vicky whispered. Tears filled her eyes.

Matt stared out at the quiet ocean. "I wish I'd met you sooner." His voice was bleak. "Things might have been different."

He felt her suppress a sob. Releasing her, he stepped back and tilted her face up. Tears glistened on her cheeks.

"Don't cry about it," he said softly. Pulling a handkerchief from his pocket, he handed it to her. "Come on, let's go get a drink."

They found a path up from the beach, and soon

were walking through the little town on their way back to the hotel. Raucous Mexican music blared out at them from little bars that Vicky hadn't even noticed in the daytime. A couple of swaggering Mexican youths passed them, and Vicky was grateful for Matt's tall, strong-looking frame beside her.

In the hotel, they found more music and many people dancing. But this was a sedate crowd, and they easily discovered a quiet corner. They sank onto the plump sofa facing out toward the water, and ordered their drinks. The dancers swirled around them. Matt's light conversation soon made Vicky feel more at ease. At last she said, "I'd better get upstairs and let Rosa go home."

"But I was just getting up the courage to ask you to dance!" Matt protested.

Vicky laughed. "How soon they forget! That boy will be up at the crack of dawn. I might just send him down the hall to pound on your door."

"Okay, okay!" Matt threw up his hands in mock surrender. "I'll get the check."

At her door, Vicky reached up and quickly kissed him. "I'm sorry, Matt."

"It's okay. See you tomorrow."

The next day at breakfast, Ben ate his scrambled eggs while he eagerly told Vicky, "Mom, I learned to count in Mexican last night."

"It's Spanish, honey," she said a little absently, while she sipped at the strong, sweet coffee.

"Right," Ben went on. Holding up one finger, he chirped, *"Uno,"* then counted off, *"dos, tres, cato."*

"Cuatro," Vicky corrected him with a fond glance.

"Cuatro, cinco. I can't remember the rest."

"That's pretty good. Did you like Rosa?"

"Yeah," Ben said enthusiastically. "She sang me a song."

Just then, Matt appeared from the lobby and joined them.

"Sounds like you'd better brush up on your singing," he said to Vicky as he sat down. "What do you have on tap for today?"

"Well," Vicky started slowly, obviously reluctant to suggest something in front of Ben that they might not be able to get out of later.

"Go ahead," Matt reassured her. "I'm ready for anything."

"I thought we might get some horses to ride. I'm sure Ben could fit on one of our saddles."

"Oh boy! Horses!" yelled Ben.

"Sounds great to me too," Matt responded with a grin. "Could I just have a cup of coffee first?"

The horses they found were a bit skinny, but seemed gentle enough. The eager Mexican boy assured them that they knew all the paths. "Very strong *caballos, señor*," he said with enthusiasm, as Matt looked dubiously at the beasts. Soon they were mounted and away, with Ben happily perched on the front of Matt's roomy saddle.

They crossed under the toll road and headed up into the rolling hills that marked the beginning of the string of scrawny mountains down the spine of Baja California. Stopping for a moment, they looked down on the panorama. Both highways and the town were spread out below them, and beyond, the blue Pacific stretched out to the horizon. Along the undulating coast to the south, they could see red-tiled roofs. Clumps of little, tightly packed houses were separated by broad expanses of windblown bluff. The sight of developers eating up the natural terrain usually made Vicky sad, but here it didn't look as though things were progressing very rapidly. One long, white stucco wall protected only a vast, open field, and the wall was already crumbling here and there. Realtors south of the border didn't seem to have the instant success they enjoyed farther north. Maybe there would still be substantial stretches of uninterrupted coastline here for years to come.

The scruffy brush beside the trail quivered. Out popped a jackrabbit. He stopped for a moment, staring, and then darted across in front of them. Ben's eyes widened in amazement. "A bunny! Mom, did you see the bunny?"

"Yes, honey, I did. He was big, wasn't he?"

"Wow! A big bunny!" Ben muttered to himself, obviously storing up this priceless memory to take home.

The horses clomped along, the sound of their hoofbeats deadened by the thick dust. They came to a fork in the path. In front of him, Matt saw Vicky stiffen in her saddle.

"Matt?" she said in a shaky voice.

He followed her gaze. Near the path, on a large rock, a rattlesnake lay sunning himself.

"Take it easy," Matt said calmly. "Just take that other path down to the beach."

As Vicky carefully guided her horse onto the descending trail, the rattler watched her with unblinking eyes. Matt waited until Vicky had gone ahead a safe distance, then he held Ben tightly and spurred his horse into a jolting trot down past the rock. He looked back over his shoulder. The snake had disappeared.

They crossed back under the toll road, and headed toward the beach. A light breeze blew up little whitecaps on the waves. Several men fished from the shore and, far out to sea, a large sailboat made its way south to Ensenada.

The horses walked contentedly along the hard-packed sand at the water's edge. Vicky pointed at a group of pelicans swooping low over the waves. Suddenly, one of them halted in midair. He pointed himself straight down, wings tucked and dropping like a rock. His wings fluttered as he splashed headfirst. Then he sat floating on the water, his underbeak bulging with fish, as he ate. In a moment he was flapping for takeoff and was soaring again, peering intently seaward for his next catch.

"I just love watching the pelicans," Vicky said to Matt as he halted beside her.

Ben added knowledgeably, "They're just like the ones we have at home."

After they had returned their horses, Matt said, "How about some lunch? I'm starving."

"I'm starving too, Mom," said Ben.

"Okay, you two!" Vicky laughed. "I know a great place to eat—at least I think I can still find it."

They piled into the van and headed south along the coast, passing an old trailer park, with its salt-stained sign, and the walled development they'd seen from the hillside.

"It should be right along here," Vicky said. "As I recall, it's a green concrete-block building behind a house off on a little dirt drive. It's called Chuey's, but I can't remember if there's a sign."

They found the restaurant perched on a bluff by the sea at the end of a rutted track. Inside, Chuey's looked as if it had been furnished with leftovers from a midwestern diner of the fifties. Formica-topped tables and unmatched chairs filled the single room, and a service counter ran along one side. It was about half full of informally dressed people—Mexicans and a scattering of transplanted Americans. None of them paid much attention to the flies circling lazily overhead.

Chuey's wife, a dark-haired American woman, was filling plates with hamburgers for a group of giggling teenagers. Chuey himself was overseeing a vat of steaming *langostas*, the big local lobsters. He was a tall, brown-skinned man with thick iron-gray hair, and his Indian heritage showed clearly in his strong nose and somber expression.

"Chuey's has the best hamburgers in the world," Vicky said. "Just walking in here makes me remember how they taste."

"The lobsters look pretty good too," said Matt, glancing at a table where two men were cracking lobster claws. "We probably won't have much of a dinner tonight—that's a good excuse for a big meal now!"

They ordered two lobsters for themselves and a hamburger for Ben. When the meal arrived, huge french fries were heaped up on the plates.

"This is a feast!" Matt opened a bottle of Carta Blanca for Vicky and a Dos Eques for himself. "Maybe Chuey would like to take in some permanent boarders."

Vicky grinned, her mouth full of lobster, butter

dripping down her chin. Ben wolfed his hamburger while gazing in admiration at the men at the next table. Their high-heeled cowboy boots, though scuffed and dusty, were covered with fancy stitching and had beautiful curved tops, and their ten-gallon hats were hung on the extra chair. Ben looked as if he would give anything to look like that.

As they were leaving, Vicky stopped to speak to Chuey's wife. "It's just as terrific as I remembered it from five years ago."

"Good." She smiled. "You should come back more often!"

Vicky laughed. "I'll do my best." Chuey looked up and gave them one of his rare smiles.

Driving slowly back toward the hotel, they saw a crowd of people standing in a field just off the road. A motley assortment of cars was parked haphazardly to one side.

"What do you suppose is going on?" Vicky wondered aloud.

Matt pulled off the road and slowed to a stop. "I don't know. Let's go find out."

A cheer went up from the crowd as they walked across the dusty field. A soccer game was in progress. A few people sat on rickety bleachers, while most of the crowd stood around the sidelines. A couple of young men moved over slightly to make room for Vicky and Ben.

Matt watched with interest for a moment, then turned to Vicky. "Could you find out what the score is, and which team is which?"

Vicky laughed helplessly. "I don't know how to say that in Spanish—I don't even know the word for 'team.'"

Matt tapped the man next to him on the shoulder.

Then he pointed to one end of the field. "Rosarito?" he asked.

The young man shook his head and pointed to the other goal. "Rosarito *alli*."

"Vicky, how do you say 'how much'?"

"Cuanto?" she guessed with a shrug.

The young man smiled enthusiastically. "Rosarito *cinco*—" he held up five fingers— *"los otros, tres."* Holding up three fingers of the other hand, he chuckled and turned back to the game.

Matt explained to Vicky, "It looks like the guys in white shirts are the home team, and they're winning five to three." He broke off to watch an attempted goal. "Oh, nice fake! He really got fooled that time."

Vicky stood with her hand resting lightly on Ben's head. Her attention was not really on the game; she was looking with interest at the spectators, who seemed to range from teenagers to sturdy, weatherbeaten old men. Suddenly her eye was caught by a flash of bright red. The man in the patterned shirt whom she had seen yesterday on the beach was standing on the other side of the playing field. I wonder why I keep seeing that guy, she thought, squinting to make sure it was the same man. It must be, because of that gaudy shirt.

Ben squirmed forward a little to get a better view of the referee he kept waiting eagerly to hear the whistle again. Matt grasped her shoulder and pointed onto the field.

"Now watch this guy he's really good. He tried this play once before. See that other guy? Okay! Nice pass! Now he's gonna set up his kick—watch the big guy in the red shirt—no, he's too late. Beautiful kick!" The crowd around them erupted into cheers. "Oh, that was a classic play. That guy is really good."

The young man next to him pointed to the player

who had just scored. "Gonzales," he said, grinning.

"*Bueno!*" Matt was getting caught up in the hometown excitement, and the young man laughed appreciatively.

"*Sí, sí, muy bueno!*"

Vicky glanced down—Ben wasn't there! She looked around hastily—no sign of a small boy with red hair.

A fight had broken out on the field. Three of the Rosarito team members were slugging it out with five or six of the visitors. The crowd screamed in mingled rage and delight. With cheers and boos they pressed forward, spilling onto the field.

Vicky found herself being moved forward with the surging mass of spectators. She grabbed Matt's arm.

"I can't find Ben! He's gone!"

Matt put an arm around her shoulders and planted his feet firmly, holding himself and Vicky still as people eddied around them.

"Calm down, Vicky. He can't have gone far. He must have gotten separated from you in this mess."

She looked around wildly. The man in the palm-patterned shirt was about ten feet away, looking at her and Matt.

The fight seemed to be over, and the crowd began drifting back behind the sidelines. Vicky pulled away and moved back farther, finally breaking free of the crowd completely.

Almost running, she moved along the back edge of the crowd, calling Ben's name. And suddenly she saw him, near a knot of young men, looking confused and scared.

"Ben!"

"Mommy!"

She ran to him and swept him up.

"Where were you, Mom? I couldn't find you. I was calling you."

"I'm right here, honey. But where did you go?"

"I was looking at the man with the whistle. And then you weren't there." He was calmer now.

"Okay, sweetie, you just got lost in the crowd. It's okay now."

Matt came up behind her. "I think it's time to move along. Let's go get the van."

Vicky shot him a grateful look. He swung Ben up on his shoulders. "Point the way to the van, Señor Ben."

They stopped along the road at one of the houses whose dusty front yards were filled with colorful pots of all sizes. After a lengthy discussion in improvised sign language, Matt pulled out a ten-dollar bill and handed it to the woman. Three small boys then appeared and began loading pots into the van. Matt was astounded at the number of pots he seemed to have bought. Vicky was delighted. *"Muchas gracias, señora!"* she called as they pulled back onto the highway.

At the hotel, Vicky packed quickly and went downstairs. Ben wanted to say goodbye to Rosa, so he and his mother went in search of her in the kitchen while Matt paid the bill. Then they went out to the van in the courtyard. Vicky helped Ben up and turned around for a last look at the grand old hotel. Slouched in a doorway was the man in the red-patterned shirt. He was wearing dark glasses, but he seemed to be staring at the van. Vicky turned away quickly, unwilling to betray her sudden feeling of unease. It's almost as if he's following us, she thought. Then she climbed into the van.

"All aboard for Los Angeles!" Matt said as he started the van and drove out under the archway.

The border crossing in this direction was not the easy process it had been the other way. They threaded through the middle of Tijuana, which looked tawdry and sleazy after the charm of Rosarito. As usual at the end of a weekend, cars were backed up for half a mile at the gates. Six lanes were open and the customs officials were moving things along as fast as possible. But drivers shifted from one sloppy line to another, looking for the quickest way through, as tourists returning from vacation mingled with Mexicans holding U.S. work permits, who had been home visiting their families for the weekend.

As the van inched forward, they watched the vendors hawking last-minute tourist souvenirs. Matt said, "This stuff is amazing!" Day-glo desert scenes painted on black velvet, many-branched candelabra made of papier mâché, wooden crucifixes whose plastic Christ figures dripped realistic plastic blood, and a vast array of piñatas, pots, and crudely worked leather goods. Every young vendor had a pile of straw sombreros heaped on his head; the ball fringe and straw flowers wobbled as they walked from car to car, and strings of sandals bumped against their backs. "What a circus!" Matt exclaimed in astonishment.

Vicky watched with amusement as the man in the car next to them haggled over a burro piñata for his daughter in the back seat. Then the cars in front of him moved forward and he stepped on the gas, cutting off an old two-tone Chevy with fake-fur upholstery that was trying to crowd ahead of him. The vendor, trotting alongside, completed the transaction and thrust the piñata through the window. Matt's van was still stopped dead, and as the next car pulled even with them, Vicky glanced at the driver. It was the man in the red-patterned shirt.

Vicky's hand tightened unconsciously on Ben's arm as she stared at the man. He met her eyes impassively, then looked straight ahead and sat revving the engine of his white '59 Plymouth.

Vicky turned to Matt. "See that man in the car next to us?" Matt looked over and nodded. "I saw him four or five times in Rosarito Beach. I think he's following us."

"Oh, come on, Vicky. Everyone's following us—they're all trying to cross the border tonight."

"No," she said quietly. "He was hanging around the hotel courtyard when we were leaving. He must have jumped into his car as soon as we took off to get here this fast."

"So?" The cars ahead moved and Matt pulled forward a few feet. "The guy probably works in San Diego. Rosarito's a small town—you could have seen lots of people more than once. Don't start imagining things."

I'm not imagining it, Vicky thought. But then they were at the border and a customs official was asking what they had bought. A few moments later, the van was on the highway, speeding north to L.A.

Outside San Diego, they stopped at a Burger King. Then Ben crawled into the back and fell asleep as they rejoined the highway.

Matt reached over and ruffled Vicky's hair. "This was a good weekend, Vicky. I'm glad we went to Mexico."

"Me too. Thanks for a really super time."

Matt twirled an imaginary mustache. "Think

nothing of it, my dear," he intoned in a mock-sinister voice, then went on more seriously, "Besides, I've been camping out at your house, eating all your food. It's the least I could do."

"Don't be silly."

They drove in silence for a while. Then Matt said, "You know, this is the first time in a long while that I've been able to really talk to someone. I'm a secretive sort of person."

"Well," Vicky said reflectively, "sometimes it's easier to open up with people when you're away from your own surroundings. Lots of times I've wished I weren't so closed off and defensive. But it's really tough so many people seem to want to pretend that I don't have Ben. They don't accept him as an integral part of my life. You seem to understand that."

"Well," he said easily, "he's a terrific kid."

"It's nice for me to see how well the two of you get along," Vicky said. "He really likes you."

After a moment, Matt said in an altered tone, "I wish I didn't know he was Tom's kid."

Vicky didn't know how to react. That's a strange thing to say, she thought. I wonder what he means.

Matt gave her hand a quick squeeze. "Tom was a lucky guy, Vicky. I hope he appreciated you."

Oh dear, Vicky thought. Why is life so complicated? And what's the matter with me? Here I am with an attractive man whose company I enjoy, and I freeze up as soon as he kisses me. I'm a grown woman with a child, and it's not as if Matt is raping me at gunpoint. Why am I getting so knotted up over this?

Vicky's sigh turned into a yawn. The wheels humming on the blacktop and the gentle, steady motion were making her feel drowsy. As she dozed off, she thought: But I do like you, Matt London.

She woke up as the van pulled into her driveway. Her head was resting against Matt's shoulder.

"Wake up, sleepyhead," he said softly in her ear. "We're home." As she sat up, he went on, "Go on and open the door. I'll carry Ben in."

Vicky stumbled sleepily up the steps and unlocked the door. Switching on the hall light, she held the door open as Matt carried her sleeping son into the house and straight through to his bedroom. She peeled off Ben's T-shirt and shorts and tucked him gently into bed. Closing his door, she went out into the hall.

"He didn't even wake up," she said. Matt smiled.

Walking into the living room, she turned on a lamp—and stared in horror. The room was in chaos. All the books and papers had been yanked out and strewn over the floor and furniture. The drawers of the desk were overturned on the floor, and their contents scattered.

"My God! Someone's broken in!" She looked around helplessly.

"Jesus!" Matt stared at the destruction. Then he said briskly, "Check and see what's missing. I'm going to call the cops."

Vicky walked slowly to her bedroom, afraid of what she would find. It too was in total disorder—her few pieces of jewelry dumped on the bed, the drawers and closet shelves emptied on the floor. She sifted through the jewelry; it all seemed to be there.

She checked the kitchen. The drawers were in disarray, as if someone had pawed through them, but again, nothing appeared to be missing.

Vicky wandered back to the living room and sat down. "I can't understand it. It looks like they didn't take anything."

When the police arrived, they asked a lot of questions that didn't shed any light. Finally Vicky said, "It's pretty weird to break into a house in this area—there's not much to steal. But it's even weirder to break in and just mess the place up without taking *anything*."

The older policeman said, "Let's make sure there's nothing missing, ma'am. Just walk slowly through the house and try to picture the way it usually looks. Sometimes that reminds you of what's missing."

Vicky obediently walked through the rooms of the little house. In her own bedroom she stopped, frowning.

"Tom's picture!" She turned to the policeman. "A photo of my husband, in a little silver frame." She looked around in bewilderment. "It's crazy! Why would someone steal Tom's picture?"

Chapter 6

"'Bye, Mom!" Ben climbed into the familiar Meadowlark minibus. Vicky came back inside and closed the door.

"Matt?"

"I'm in the kitchen."

She went in to find him rinsing the breakfast dishes. "You don't have to do that," she said distractedly. Wandering back to the living room, she began leafing through the stack of papers she'd piled on the coffee table the night before. With a sigh, she picked up the whole pile and carried it to the desk, setting it down next to another untidy heap. She look around aimlessly.

Matt walked into the room. "Aren't you going to be late for work?"

"I know. I should get out of here. But I can't seem to get myself going. I feel funny about leaving the house."

"Well..." Matt began.

"I just can't understand the whole thing," Vicky went on nervously. "What was the point of it? Breaking in and making all this mess, and then all they took was Tom's picture."

"It is pretty mysterious," Matt agreed. "But Vicky, they certainly won't be coming back, if that's what's bothering you. They had the whole weekend. The best thing for you to do is go to work and get things back to normal."

"You're right." Vicky stood indecisively in the middle of the room.

"Do you want me to stick around here today? Would that make you feel better?"

"No, no," she said quickly. "That's ridiculous. Mrs. Garfield's coming over to meet Ben, and you wouldn't get anything done." Vicky picked up her bag from the chair and slung it over her shoulder, now moving briskly and in control of herself. "No," she went on. "You go on and get some pages written." He followed her into the kitchen and watched her take a foil-covered package out of the freezer. "We'll have meatloaf tonight. See you later."

"Vicky?"

She turned, her hand on the doorknob.

"You okay?"

She gave him a grateful smile. "Sure. See you tonight."

Mrs. Garfield heard the minibus pull up in front of the house. She walked to the door, then stood waiting for a few moments. When she opened it, Ben was standing expectantly on the step.

"Hi, Ben!"

"I won today!" he crowed.

"You sure did." She shook her head in mock dismay. "You're getting too fast for me."

He came in, chattering about what had gone on at school that morning. At last she said, "It's such a nice day. Where shall we go, the beach or the park?"

"The park," he decided. "This time will you push me real high on the swings?"

"As high as I can," she said, laughing.

They walked up the street toward the park. At the intersection, Mrs. Garfield said, "What do we do here, Ben?"

He chanted, "Stop, look, and listen before you cross the street. Use your eyes, use your ears, then use your feet."

"That's right," she said approvingly. "We look both ways and hold hands when we cross."

Skipping along beside her, he confided, "I learned how to count in Spanish. Wanna hear? *Uno, dos, tres*—I forget the next one."

"That's real good. Now, how high can you count in English?"

When they reached the park, Mrs. Garfield settled herself on a sunny bench and took out her knitting. Ben ran to join some other kids in the sandbox. After a time, he came over and said, "I'm ready to go on the swing now." As she pushed, he shouted, "Higher! Higher!," laughing shrilly as she complied.

A group of older children arrived and piled onto the revolving platform in the corner of the park. "I wanna go on the merry-go-round," Ben demanded immediately.

Mrs. Garfield looked over; the big kids were leaning out dangerously as it spun around.

"All right," she said, "but you have to hold on tight. No tricks, now."

"Okay." He trotted to the merry-go-round and the kids obligingly stopped it so he could climb on. Then one of the boys started pushing it again, running faster and faster and finally leaping on with a bump.

Mrs. Garfield picked up her knitting.

—Thank goodness those kids are here. I'm sure as shootin' too old to push that thing around. Makes me dizzy just watching.

After a while, Ben came over to the bench and stood next to her. "Ready to go home?" Mrs. Garfield asked. He nodded. "Fine. I've got a nice surprise for you back at the house." Ben's eyes lit up.

"A surprise?"

"Yes, indeedy. I baked a whole batch of peanut butter cookies. You can have some with your milk when we get home."

They left the park and walked slowly down the hill.

"I rode on a horse," Ben told her suddenly.

Mrs. Garfield was used to these bold announcements. "That's nice. While you were in Mexico?" she asked.

"Yes. And Mom rode one too. Mr. Matt had a brown horse and Mom had one with spots."

"Good."

"We saw a big bunny."

"On your ride?"

"Yes. We rode on the beach and my horse got his feet wet."

"That sounds like fun."

"I'm gonna ask Mom if I can have a horse."

Mrs. Garfield smiled down at Ben. "Well, I don't think a horse would be very happy in your yard, Ben.

It's too small. But I'll bet you can ride one again when you go back to Mexico."

They reached the corner of Seaview and West Channel, and stopped. Even though Seaview was a short, quiet cross-street, Mrs. Garfield took Ben's hand. Without prompting, Ben began, "Stop, look, and listen." They finished the jingle together and then stepped off the curb.

Mrs. Garfield heard the roaring engine and squealing tires. She quickly glanced over her shoulder. A large, dark car screamed around the corner. It was almost on top of them.

They had nearly reached the safety of the sidewalk. She thrust Ben in front of her. "Run, Ben!" she cried, and pushed him forward with all her might.

There was a sickening thud as the car hit Mrs. Garfield. It roared on down the street and screeched around the corner, heading for the highway.

Faces appeared at windows up and down the street. The young man in the blond ponytail dashed out of his house. He saw Ben getting up off the sidewalk where he'd fallen. The child was crying and had a skinned knee, but at least he was standing up on his own. The car must have missed him. The woman still lay in the crosswalk. Several motorists had stopped by now, and an elderly man came carefully out of his house saying, "I've called an ambulance. They should be right along."

The young man knelt down by Mrs. Garfield. There was little blood that he could see. Gingerly he pressed his forefingers against her neck. He hoped the pulse he felt was hers and not his own, pounding through his body.

A woman came over, carrying a blanket from the

back of her car. "Here, put this over her. I don't think you should try to move her or anything."

The young man gratefully stepped aside and let her take charge. He moved quickly to the sidewalk. Scooping Ben up in his arms, he asked, "You okay, kid?" Then, trying to comfort Ben, he stood there waiting for the ambulance and the police.

Almost an hour later, Vicky's little red beetle turned onto Seaview. She parked in front of her own house and then trotted down the sidewalk to the blond man's door. He had Ben by the hand as he came onto the porch. Ben had a couple of Band-Aids clumsily patched on his knees, and a Fudgesicle in his hand.

Vicky knelt and put her arms around him. "Oh, honey, you okay?" she crooned in his ear.

"Yeah. Peter bought me a Fudgesicle and Mrs. Garfield got hurt. She went to the hospital in an ambulance."

Vicky smiled shakily at the young man. "I can't thank you enough for bringing Ben home with you and taking care of him. Poor Mrs. Garfield. Did you see what happened?"

"No, I didn't, but it was hit-and-run for sure."

"Well, thank you again. I'm sure glad you were here." Vicky took Ben by the hand. "We're going to see Mrs. Garfield in the hospital."

The hospital information desk didn't yet have a room number for Mrs. Garfield, but the attendant there said she'd probably be on the fifth floor. When Vicky got up there, she talked to the floor nurse. Mrs. Garfield was just being settled in her room; she had a broken shoulder and a less serious break in her lower right leg, as well as some cracked ribs and a mild concussion.

"Oh my God!" Vicky breathed.

The nurse said cheerfully, "Oh, it's not as bad as it sounds. Actually, she was lucky not to have any internal injuries. She'll be home in a week or so, I expect. But I don't think you should go in and see her now she's still pretty groggy and she ought to just go off to sleep. Why don't you call tomorrow and see how she's doing?"

"All right, but isn't there something I can do now?"

"Well, perhaps you can tell me " She pulled out a typewritten form. "We don't know who to get in touch with. Do you know if she has a family?"

"She's a widow, but she has a son in Detroit. His name is Ed I'm not sure if it's Edward or Edgar, but anyway, it's Ed Garfield. He must be in the Detroit phone book."

"Fine," the nurse said briskly. "We'll try to locate him. In any case, she'll be able to tell us herself tomorrow."

Vicky told her she'd be happy to pick up Mrs. Garfield's keys the next day, and stop by her house for her toothbrush and a couple of nightgowns. "Tell her I'll call tomorrow," she said as she walked toward the elevator.

Driving home, Vicky was extra careful, unusually aware of the damage a car could do. She made a cautious right turn from the highway onto West Channel. Then she stiffened and her hands gripped the wheel tightly. The Mexican man who had been following them was just entering a neighborhood liquor store! He was wearing a plain green shirt, not the red-palm pattern, but she was certain it was the same man.

Vicky zoomed the few blocks to her house. Jumping out of the car, she hustled Ben inside. Matt looked up from his book.

"Hi! Wow, your neighbor told me about the accident. It sounds—"

Vicky rushed past him to the phone. "Wait a minute, I have to call the police." She dialed and waited.

"Hello, this is Mrs. Hunter of 19 Seaview Avenue. My housekeeper, Mrs. Florence Garfield, was run down in a hit-and-run accident this afternoon, and I've just seen the driver who hit her!"

She listened for a moment, then went on, "He was going into that liquor store on West Channel, just a couple of doors from the Coast Highway—yes, the south side of West Channel. He's Mexican, kind of heavy, and he's wearing a green shirt." Another pause. "Oh, about fifty, I think. Okay, yes, thank you." She hung up and turned to Matt. "I just saw that guy who followed us from Rosarito Beach. He must have been trying to hit Ben. The police are going to pick him up. Now we'll find out what this is all about!" She looked at him triumphantly.

"Are you sure it's the same guy?" Matt asked slowly.

"Yes, positive."

He followed her out to the kitchen. "But even if it is, what makes you think he was involved in the hit-and-run?"

"Well, he didn't follow us all the way up here for nothing," she said reasonably. "It can't be coincidence that the day after he follows us home, someone tries to

118

run Ben down in the street. I just hope they catch him."

"I hope you're right," Matt said dubiously.

They were just finishing dinner when the phone rang.

"I'll get it." Vicky pushed back her chair, leaving Matt and Ben at the table.

She returned a few moments later, her eyes gleaming. "Well, they've got him. They want me to come to the station to identify him. I'll just throw these dishes into the dishwasher..."

Matt was on his feet. "I'll help you. Then we can all go together. You're not driving there by yourself."

"Where are we going?" Ben asked.

"We're taking a ride," Matt told him. "Why don't you go and get your sweatshirt?"

As Matt drove along San Vicente Boulevard, the summer sunset blazed behind them in glorious Technicolor.

"We'll go across on Federal to Santa Monica, and then it's just a few more blocks toward the freeway," Vicky said. Matt followed her directions, turning left on Santa Monica. "Now what?" he asked.

"It's 1663 Butler, but I don't think we can turn on Butler. Go on to Purdue and make a right."

They pulled into the parking lot and went into the West L.A. police station.

"I'm Mrs. Hunter. Sergeant Victor told me to come and identify someone," Vicky announced to the policeman at the desk. The lobby of the station was a small, enclosed room with a couple of wooden benches.

"Do you want us to come in with you?" Matt asked.

Vicky tousled Ben's hair and said, "No, I don't think so. Maybe you and Ben could go out and look at the cars or the fountain or something. I don't imagine I'll be too long."

"Oh, I think Ben and I can find plenty to amuse ourselves with," he assured her. "Good luck."

The desk sergeant buzzed open the door to the guts of the station, and Vicky disappeared inside. Along one wall were a number of small cubicle offices, while inside the main room some desks were occupied by policemen and policewomen on the phone, typing up reports, and leafing through the sports section of the paper. A swarthy man in uniform came out of one of the cubicles.

"Mrs. Hunter?"

"Yes," said Vicky. "Is he in there?"

"Yes. But before I take you in, I'd like to discuss with you what you saw. This man, Pedro Esteban, claims that he's a gardener in the Rustic Canyon area and that he was working when the accident occurred. In fact, he says that when we picked him up, he was waiting for a ride from a friend because his pickup is being repaired and he had no other means of transportation. Now, we've checked this out with the East L.A. division where he lives, and so far his story holds up. What exactly did you see when the accident occurred?"

"Oh, I didn't see the accident," Vicky said. She saw his look of dismay and hurried on, "But I'm sure he's the one who did it. You may not know it, but there have been a whole string of attacks against myself and my son. First, he and I were run off the road and almost killed. Then Ben was lured to a pool and almost drowned. When I returned from spending last weekend in Mexico, I found that my house had been broken into. And now, today, my babysitter was run down in an attempt to hit my child. This man was hanging around us and acting suspicious the whole time we were in Rosarito Beach, and then he followed us across the border and all the way to L.A. It's obvious that he's mixed up in this whole business. I'm just glad you caught him."

Sergeant Victor shook his head and sighed. "Yes, ma'am. Well, let's have you take a look at him, since you're here."

He preceded her to the door and opened it, ushering Vicky inside. The dark-haired man in the green shirt glared up at both of them from his chair. A young policeman stood lounging against the far wall.

Vicky looked at the man in the chair. Now she could see him from about the same angle as she had at the border, looking down into the Plymouth from the van. The man continued to stare up at her belligerently. Vicky felt the blood rise in her face. She turned to the sergeant behind her. "Could we talk outside?"

He opened the door and politely escorted her out, closing the door behind him. Vicky faced him, still flushed. "I don't know how to say this..." she began. Then she blurted out the rest of it. "That's not the same man I saw in Mexico. I thought he was, on the street. But now I realize that I've never seen him before. I'm awfully sorry."

Looking resigned and annoyed, the sergeant led Vicky to the front of the station. "I'm really sorry," Vicky said again.

"That's all right," he replied wearily.

The lobby gate clicked conclusively behind her. She went outside to the street. Matt and Ben were standing by a police car. They came toward her.

"Well, what happened?" Matt asked.

Vicky took Ben's hand and looked down at him, avoiding Matt's eyes. "It wasn't the same guy."

"Oh."

They drove home in a silence relieved only by Ben's animated chatter about the police cars. When they got there, Vicky whisked Ben into the bathtub and then into bed. She closed his door firmly and walked into the living room.

"Well, that does it. I'm leaving. I'm going to pack up and get Ben out of here. Even if it wasn't the same man, somebody tried to run Ben over today. And they're not going to get another chance." She turned on her heel and went out the front door.

Matt followed, to find her pulling suitcases down from the shelves at the back of the garage. "Wait a minute, Vicky. Let's think this through."

"I've already thought it through, and we're leaving. I've had enough of this." Pushing past Matt, she lugged the two big cases across the yard and into the house. Dumping one in the living room, she took the other into her bedroom and opened it on the bed.

Matt stood in the doorway and watched her yank open a drawer. She lifted out a pile of shirts and jammed them into the suitcase. He said quietly, "I think this whole business is getting a little out of proportion. You're letting your imagination run away with you."

She whirled to face him. "You sound just like those cops," she hissed furiously. "I know you think I'm being totally paranoid and crazy, but he's not your kid. I wouldn't expect you to understand." She elbowed him out of the way and stalked back to the living room.

She went to the desk and began sorting through the papers, pulling out her bank book and other valuables and tossing them into the suitcase. Matt trailed after her.

"Now, Vicky," he began.

"Don't 'Now, Vicky' me. I know what I'm doing."

"But you can't just wake Ben up and drive off into the night," he protested. "Where are you going to go?"

"I can do whatever I decide is best." Vicky dropped another armful of papers into the suitcase and stood glaring at Matt. "Now, if you don't mind, I'm going to wash my hair and get ready to leave. If it's not too much trouble, you can make sure nothing happens to my son while I'm in the shower." She stormed down the hall and into the bathroom.

Turning on the water, she undressed and stared into the little mirror. Why can't he see that we've got to get out of here? I'd think he could understand, she reflected bitterly. She stepped into the shower and began scrubbing herself violently.

—What do I really know about him, anyway? I don't even know if he's really who he claims to be—he never talks about his college days with Tom. And it was just as he showed up out of the blue that all these horrible things started happening.

Vicky poured shampoo into her palm and started lathering her hair.

—Maybe he *is* involved somehow in whatever is behind all this. That policewoman who came when Ben fell in the pool certainly sounded suspicious. And now that I think about it, I *didn't* see what happened at the pool. He could have pushed Ben in before I got there—maybe Matt was holding him underwater instead of pulling him out. For all I know, he's trying to get me to stay here so he can murder us both in the middle of the night.

She finished rinsing her hair and turned off the water. Leaning over, she wrapped a towel around her head. I guess I don't really believe that, she thought. Remembering the weekend in Mexico and all the time they'd spent together here, she shook her head. I couldn't be that wrong about him.

Drying her hair vigorously, she combed it in front of the mirror. I guess it is pretty stupid to go charging out in the middle of the night. She made a face at herself in the mirror. Matt's right, I am overreacting. I sounded like a certifiable nut case.

Vicky wrapped her robe around herself and walked slowly into the living room. "I'm sorry, Matt," she said in a small voice.

Matt jumped off the couch and took her hands. "It's okay."

"No, it's not. I said all those mean things to you, and there I was running around like a madwoman—"

Matt's mouth closed on hers; he kissed her long and hard. Then he held her close, feeling her tremble against him. "Take it easy." He drew her down to the couch.

She sat there, her head in her hands, wishing the whole problem would just go away. But it wouldn't. Finally she said, "Matt? Even though I haven't been sounding exactly rational, all these things really *have* been happening. You see that, don't you?"

"Yes," he said slowly. "I can understand how you feel. But there's still a chance that it's all been a bizarre string of accidents and coincidences. Besides, there isn't a whole lot you can do."

"Well, I've been thinking. Maybe I should quit my job and take Ben out of school and simply stay with him all the time."

"Oh, Vicky, I don't think that's a very good idea." Matt's voice was gentle. "You'll scare Ben and make him terribly confused. When he's in school, there are a lot of people around. It's good for him to spend time with other kids. Besides, I'll be here."

Vicky looked at him, almost convinced. Matt continued, "I'm moving my stuff in and I'll just work here. That way, I'll be around all the time and you won't have to worry about Ben. I'll watch him when he gets home from school."

"Oh, Matt," Vicky sighed.

He pulled her closer. She could feel the steady thumping of his heart as he gently kissed her.

Chapter 7

Vicky helped Ben get dressed for school. Her tall slender frame moved gracefully about his room as she handed him a pair of long pants. "I found that note you brought home from school yesterday. You're supposed to wear long pants and socks under your sneakers, no bare toes in sandals. Today your whole class is going to the park." She bent to tie his shoes. "I think it sounds like fun," she continued.

"Oh yeah, I forgot," Ben said. "We're gonna see birds and lizards."

"Good." The lines of tension on her face had been nearly erased by a good night's sleep. "Now run on out and get some breakfast. Matt's going to be here when you get home from school."

Ben started toward the door. "Mom, does Matt live here?"

Vicky hardly knew what to say, but she saw him

looking at her, waiting for an answer. Finally she said, "Yes, he does right now, but it's only for a little while."

"Oh," Ben said maturely. "It's like visiting!"

"That's right, honey." She followed him out to the kitchen.

After Ben had left for school, Vicky gathered up her things, ready to go to work. She smiled at Matt. "I feel so much better, knowing you'll be here," she told him. Then she linked her arms around his neck and lifted her face to kiss him.

"Don't worry about a thing." He touched her hair and then her cheek, and stood at the door to watch her go.

When she reached her office, Vicky picked up the phone and dialed the hospital. While she waited to be connected to Mrs. Garfield's room, she thought: Maybe I'll have time to run out at lunchtime and get her some flowers. Then if it's okay with her, I'll stop by the hospital on my way home. That way I can pick up her house keys, and then tonight I can pack a little bag for her and drop it off tomorrow. I wonder what she'd like to read.

Mrs. Garfield came on the line. "Oh, hello, Mrs. Garfield. How are you feeling?"

Ten children under the age of five descended on Will Rogers Park in a state of excitement. The two young teachers marshaled their charges, and the group proceeded up from the parking lot to the grassy space in front of the ranch house.

"Now remember, kids, what we talked about—everyone stays together. Okay?"

"Okay." A chorus of eager young voices echoed him.

They set off across the grass, past the front of the ranch house. Bill, the younger teacher, walked in front, and Wendy brought up the rear, shooing the stragglers along.

"That house is where Will Rogers used to live. This whole area was his ranch a long time ago," Wendy explained. "See that low building up ahead? That used to be a stable. Now it's the Nature Center. We're going there first."

A wooden sign was hung on the wall by the door of the Nature Center. On it were the names of a number of wild animals found in the park, and pictures of their paw prints.

Bill pointed to the sign. "These are the footprints of the animals they have here in the park. Inside, they have pictures of the animals."

As the kids entered the small center, the variety of open exhibits caught their attention. There were rocks and birds' nests sitting on low tables, inviting examination. Little hands reached out in fascination.

"Don't touch," Bill warned.

The kind-looking docent greeted them. "It's okay. That's the whole point of having the exhibits, so the children can touch them." She ushered the children past the birds' nests, urging them to touch them gently.

In the next room, a stuffed raccoon and a ground squirrel perched on top of a glass display case. "See the sign," she said to the children. "It says, 'Please pet me.'"

Wendy and Bill stood behind their little band and watched the children's expressions of awe as they took turns petting the animals.

The docent had moved to the far end of the room. "Here are some stones that the Indians used to grind up acorns. They made flour out of the nuts and baked it into bread." She looked over the tops of the children's heads to Wendy. "Usually I let the kids try grinding, but this group might be a little young for that."

"I want to try it," Ben announced.

"Me too," said his friend Jimmy.

Wendy grinned and shrugged her shoulders. "It's up to you," she said to the docent.

"Well, maybe I have a few acorns here in this bag." She put a couple of the brown nuts on the center of one of the hollowed stones. "It's pretty hard. Let me help you." She and Ben put their hands on the grinding stone and started to work.

When all the children had had their fill of grinding, petting, and looking around, Wendy and Bill thanked the docent and herded the group outside.

"We're going up to a nice grassy place to have lunch," Bill said. "Let's go. Follow me."

He started off up the trail, and most of the children scampered along after him. But Ben was staring in fascination at the horse area across from the Nature Center. A young girl was practicing jumps in the training ring in front of the stables.

"That horse is just like the one I rode," he informed Jimmy, who had also stopped to look.

"Let's keep moving, boys," Wendy urged.

"Wendy, can we ride the horses?"

"No, Ben. Those horses belong to people who keep them here, and besides, I don't think everyone knows how to ride."

"I know how," Ben assured her.

She smiled at him as he turned for a last, longing look at the beautiful creatures.

They continued up the winding trail, stopping for a

glimpse of a ground squirrel whisking out of sight. They walked under huge eucalyptus trees, whose fallen leaves and seed buttons lay everywhere underfoot.

Bill stopped and picked up one of the small, round pods. He held it out for the children to see.

"These things fall off the big trees around here—maybe you know they're eucalyptus trees. It looks kind of like a button. And guess what? The Indians used to use them for buttons on their clothes."

"Can I take some home?" Jessica was obviously planning a new set of buttons for her jacket.

"You can each take one. Put it in your pocket."

The climb grew steeper and the ground fell away sharply next to the path, down to a tangled ravine crowded with chaparral.

An elderly couple out for a stroll passed the group, but for the most part, the park was deserted on a weekday morning. When they reached the open, flat area at the top of the hill, the children threw themselves down on the sparse grass. Suddenly Bill pointed.

"Shh! Look, a lizard."

On one of the huge flat rocks that dotted the area was a tiny gray lizard. "Where?" Jimmy asked.

The lizard stared at them briefly, then scurried out of sight.

"I saw him! I saw him!" Jimmy shouted.

Wendy smiled. "It's hard to see them when they hold still, isn't it? They're almost the same color as the rocks."

Up above, hawks circled lazily, their wings spread to catch the shifting breezes.

As the children settled down for lunch, Wendy and Bill took turns telling them about the plants and animals in the park.

"Have any of you ever seen a cat with a really short, stubby tail?" Wendy asked. "That's what bobcats look like. They're a little bigger than regular housecats, and sometimes people see them here in the park. One day someone saw a cat lying beside the road on the way into the park, and he thought it was a kitty that had been hit by a car."

"Ooh," said several of the children.

"So the man went to the rangers to tell them about it, and they all went back down to see if they could take the cat to the vet. And you know what? It wasn't a hurt kitty at all—it was a wild bobcat lying in the sun sleeping," Wendy finished with a smile.

"Are there lions around here?" Becky asked with big eyes.

"Some people think so," Wendy answered. "A couple of years ago, some people saw a mountain lion in the park. And then some other people saw him way down in the woods by the beach. They think it might be the same one. But no one's seen him for a while."

"Would he come and eat us?" Becky asked, her eyes even bigger.

Wendy laughed. "No, you're all too noisy. The lion would be scared of you."

The children shrieked with laughter. Several of them pantomimed crouching, growling lions while the rest yelled and giggled.

Ben pointed to a blackened tree standing at the edge of the clearing. "Why is that tree black?"

"It's left over from the fire," Bill told him. "There was a huge fire in these mountains a while ago, and a lot of the trees were burned. The flames were really big, and the fire went clear down by the ranch house."

"Were the horses okay?" asked Ben.

"Yes, they were. But for a while, no one was sure they would be. They had to take them down into that grassy area by the house in case the fire burned their stables. But the firemen were able to save all the buildings here."

"That's why it's so important to be careful of fires in the mountains," Wendy went on. "It's very easy for the wind to spread a fire, and the dry bushes catch fire quickly. A lot of the plants have grown back since the fire, but for a while, all the ground was black and there were practically no plants anywhere."

"Wow," said Jimmy, "I bet everybody was scared."

"They sure were," said Bill. He went on to tell them how the wild animals had had to run for their lives, and that some of them had died in the fire.

"Do you think the mountain lion is okay?" asked Becky.

"Probably. Lions can run pretty fast," Wendy said. "Anyway, I hope so."

After lunch, Wendy called to the children, "Bring all your trash and put it in this bag, kids. We can't leave any litter." As they trooped over, she went on, "Now you can go look around this area, but don't get too far away. I'll be right here; make sure you can see me all the time."

"If you see any animals, move quietly," Bill added. "Otherwise you'll scare them away."

The children spread out across the open area, climbing on the rocks and picking up bits of shiny stone. Jimmy spotted a squirrel and advanced slowly toward it with an outstretched hand. "Here, squirrel!"

On an outcropping of rock at the edge of the flat space, a good-sized lizard sat blinking in the sun. Ben approached it carefully and stood gazing at it from a few feet away. Boy and lizard stared at one another without moving. Then, with a flick of its tail, the lizard turned and scuttled across the rock and down the other side.

As quietly as he could, Ben crept around the rocky protrusion. He clung to its sides as the ground sloped down toward the shallow ravine. He peered into the crevices of the rock, but saw no sign of his lizard. Then he heard it—a rustling in the dry underbrush a little farther down. He started after it cautiously, his eyes searching the ground.

"Hey, kids, come take a look at this!" Bill's voice carried over the rocks. Ben looked back. But his lizard was only a little way off.

The children gathered around Bill, who was squatting beside a mound of earth. Insects flew in and out of the tiny holes in the dirt.

"These guys are digger bees."

Several of the children stepped back hastily.

Bill said quickly, "Don't worry, these bees don't sting. They build their nest in the ground instead of up in trees. That's why they're called diggers—they dig lots of tunnels and store their food underground."

The children crowded closer to look. "Careful not to smash their house," Bill warned. "Just watch."

Ben looked and looked, but his lizard seemed to have disappeared completely. Then he heard a much louder rustling ahead of him. Beyond a couple of trees, he saw a small golden puppy with fluffy fur. It was snapping in the air and jumping around, trying to catch a butterfly. A man stood near the puppy. As Ben came closer, the man said kindly, "Do you want to pet my puppy dog?"

"Yes," said Ben eagerly. He trotted over to the

puppy and bent to touch him. "Let's take him back there under that big tree," the man said. "He's very little and it's too hot out here in the sun for him." He scooped up the puppy and carried him while Ben patiently followed. They sat down behind the trunk of a large tree. The man held out the puppy to Ben. "Would you like to hold him?"

Ben nodded excitedly and clutched the little dog in his lap. The puppy squirmed around and licked Ben's chin. Ben giggled.

The man unhooked a small canteen from his belt and unscrewed the lid. "How about a drink of water?" he said to Ben. "Bet you haven't seen one of these before. It's called a canteen, and cowboys use them for water when they're out on the range with their horses."

"I rode a horse," Ben told him proudly.

"Good," said the man. "Now you drink out of the top, just like a pop bottle. Here. Try it." He thrust the canteen into Ben's hands and helped him tilt it to his lips. "Bet that tastes good. Have all you want." He watched Ben swallow down some of the liquid, then he recapped the canteen and fastened it on his belt.

"What's the puppy's name?" Ben asked.

"I haven't thought of one yet," the man answered. "What do you think it should be?"

"Dusty," Ben answered promptly. "That's the name of the dog in my book."

"Sounds like a good name."

Ben's eyelids drooped heavily, and he blinked to keep them open. He stroked the dog. "Hi, Dusty." The puppy jumped up and licked his face. "See, he likes his name."

The man watched impatiently as Ben continued to pet the puppy and talk to it. Suddenly, Ben's eyes closed and his head dropped forward onto his chest. Swiftly the man picked Ben up and slung him over his shoulder in a fireman's carry. Then he scooped up the puppy with his free hand. Turning, he walked along the ravine, then climbed onto an overgrown, narrow trail. As he stepped through the undergrowth, Wendy's voice sounded in the distance.

"Ben? Come on, Ben. It's time to go."

The man began to breathe heavily as his long legs carried him and his burden up the winding trail. It was an area of the park that was infrequently used, and overhanging trees and scraggly bushes reached out, scratching Ben's dangling arms and slowing their progress. The warm midday sun seeped through the branches above, and beat down on them in the open spaces. The man's plaid cotton shirt was soaked under his arms and in a stripe down his back. Occasionally a group of California valley quail rose up in indignation, flapping through the brush as he tramped near their resting places.

At one point he stopped and eyed a ravine off to the left. The steep sides were covered with chaparral, but it was an impossible climb down and then back up. No, he would go on up near where he'd left the car on the fire trail. He'd spotted the place on his way down. The sides of the ravine were steep and rocky, not easily accessible even on horseback, but there was a gentler slope at the far end. A small stream trickled down through the bottom of the cut. It might draw some of the carnivorous mountain animals, and was a likely place for the rattlers that could be found all over these hills. By midafternoon, the sun would be gone from the craggy slope and the snakes would be moving around in the more temperate air. An animal rustled through the undergrowth near the path, and the man shivered. He'd be happy to unload the kid and get out of there.

At last he reached the place he'd been watching for. It had been a long two miles from where he'd picked Ben up. Leaving the trail, he pushed through the dense thickets and down into the ravine. He kept moving until the rocky slopes on either side were too sheer to climb.

The puppy whimpered as the man bent to dump Ben on the ground under an overhang of rock. He set the puppy down and pushed Ben's limp form farther in, so he couldn't be seen from above. Stepping back, he glanced around and nodded in satisfaction. He picked up the puppy. With a quick movement of his powerful hands, he broke its neck and tossed its limp body under the rocky ledge next to the unconscious boy.

Then he turned and walked rapidly out of the ravine.

Bill climbed back up over the rocky outcrop. Meeting Wendy's eyes, he spread his hands in frustration. "Nothing."

Wendy spoke quickly in a low voice. "We've got to get the rest of the kids back to school."

"Yeah," Bill said heavily.

"We'll stop and tell the rangers to come up and look for him; he can't have gone very far."

"Okay." He called to the children, "Let's go, kids."

"Wendy, where's Ben?" Jimmy's anxious face looked up at her.

"He must have wandered too far away. We're going to tell the rangers to come and find him." She tried to sound confident, but her voice was shaky. Jimmy took her hand as they started silently down the path.

Bill herded the little group past the ranch house toward the bus waiting in the parking lot. As soon as they had passed her, Wendy broke into a run. Bursting into the ranger station, she gasped out her story.

The ranger was calmly sympathetic. "We'll get up there right away and start looking. Don't worry, a kid that size can't go very far."

"Okay." Wendy swallowed hard. "We'll be back as soon as we get the other kids home. But please, call the school right away when you find him."

"Sure. He'll probably be here waiting for you."

She joined Bill in the minibus, and they headed out of the park. The children, sensing their tension, were unnaturally quiet all the way back.

When they reached the school, Wendy left Bill to sort out the kids and send them home on the appropriate buses, and quickly went to tell the school's director that Ben was missing. "You call the house and tell the babysitter, and I'll call his mother at work," the director told her. "Then get right back up to the park and find out what's going on."

Matt walked in from the yard to answer the phone, his mind still on the paragraph he'd been writing. He listened to Wendy's tightly controlled voice with mounting concern.

"Have you called Mrs. Hunter?" he asked. He nodded as he heard her reply. "Fine," he said brusquely. "Now how do I get to this park?" Wendy gave him directions, and then assured him that the rangers had everything under control.

"Right." Matt hung up and grabbed his keys. A few moments later, his blue van was backing out of Vicky's driveway.

Vicky picked up the ringing phone in her office. "Vicky Hunter, story department," she said easily. Her face drained of color and her hand clenched on the receiver as the school's director told her that Ben was lost.

"Now, Mrs. Hunter," his voice went on calmly. "I thought it best to let you know. But the park rangers are in charge now, and they assure us your son will be found in no time at all. You know how these children sometimes are—"

Vicky dropped the receiver on its cradle and frantically looked around for her purse. Fishing for her keys as she went, she ran out of her office and across the lot to her car.

White-faced and shaking, Vicky recklessly passed the cars in front of her as she sped toward Will Rogers Park. She told herself over and over that Ben would be fine. The female ranger at the gate recognized her distraught condition and waved her on. "Have they found my son?" Vicky almost screamed. The pleasant young woman shook her head.

"Not yet. But they will."

"They better!" Vicky gunned her car up the drive and careened into the parking lot.

Leaping out of the VW, she ran up toward the ranger station. Matt was standing outside, talking to the ranger. She grabbed his arm and panted, "Have they found him?"

"No, Vicky, not yet."

Her hands tightened convulsively. "What's going on? It's been almost two hours!"

Matt said quickly, "This is Mrs. Hunter," and the ranger looked at her with compassion.

"We're getting the second phase of the search under

way right now. We've been all over the immediate area on foot, but it seems your son managed to wander farther than most kids do. We're broadening the search now, and I'm sure he'll turn up before too long."

Vicky looked at Matt, her eyes bleak. "They've got him," she said tonelessly. "It's too late—they've killed him by now."

"Vicky, I—"

The ranger broke in with a frown, "Mrs. Hunter, do you have some reason to think that your son didn't just wander off?"

"Yes." She nodded hopelessly. "Someone has tried to kill him before, and now they've got him."

The ranger raised an eyebrow at Matt. "Do you know anything about this, Mr. London?"

"I'm afraid it's possible," Matt said slowly. "There has been a series of peculiar incidents involving Ben. I wouldn't rule it out."

"I see. Do you—"

"Unfortunately, I can't tell you anything helpful about who it might be. That's been the problem."

Two men on horseback reined in behind the hut. They wore blue shirts and trousers, and had badges on their sleeves. One of them called, "We're going up now, Pete. We'll cover F7 and then go on up to F8."

"Right. Hang on a minute, though." The ranger walked over to them. "That's the mother, so keep it down. She says the kid has been threatened. We may be dealing with a snatch or something."

"Oh, yeah?"

"I don't know. But if she's right, we may be looking for a body. I'll radio up to Bill; he's already up there and you'll be checking in with him."

"Right." They cantered off, and Pete returned to Matt and Vicky.

"Mrs. Hunter, those men are from the Mounted Assistance Unit. They're a highly trained volunteer group that's established just for this purpose—to find people who get lost up there. They're starting a grid search of the area, and they'll be coordinating with our own people on foot and in vehicles along the fire trails. You can take a look at the map inside the hut and you'll see how it works."

Vicky nodded speechlessly and walked slowly into the hut. Matt spoke quickly to the ranger.

"What are his chances, if he is just lost? How about snakes out here?"

Pete glanced toward the hut. "It all depends. We do have rattlesnakes, but they won't be moving around for a couple of hours yet. If the boy sticks to the trails, he should be okay, but..."

"Yeah." Matt shook his head and started toward the hut.

Vicky appeared in the doorway, her hands clenching and unclenching on her purse. "Matt, I've got to do something. I'm going up there to look for him. If he hears my voice " She broke off.

"Mrs. Hunter, I understand how you feel, but I can't let you do that," Pete told her. "They're professionals up there looking for your son, and you'd just be in the way. I'm sorry." He turned to Matt. "The most useful thing you can do is take care of Mrs. Hunter. Why don't you go over to the ranch house? I'll tell them to give you some coffee, and you can sit down. Don't worry, we'll let you know the minute we hear anything."

Matt took Vicky's arm. "He's right, Vicky. Come on, let's go drink that coffee."

She allowed him to lead her away. Her steps dragged, and she seemed to have given up. Outside the ranch house, Wendy approached them hesitantly, her face red and blotched.

"Oh, Mrs. Hunter, I've just been calling the school. I'm so terribly sorry. I feel as though it's all my fault..."

Vicky walked past her woodenly, as if she hadn't heard.

"She's pretty upset," Matt said unnecessarily. "Are you from the school?"

Wendy nodded and gulped. "I'm Ben's teacher," she whispered.

He took pity on her distress. "There's no point in your staying here. Why don't you go home? They'll notify everybody when they find him."

Wendy nodded numbly as he followed Vicky inside.

3:10 P.M.

Jack Kehoe reined in his horse. He took off his broad-brimmed blue hat and mopped his forehead.

"Jeez, it's hot," he informed his partner.

Vince Langley squinted up the trail ahead of them. "Someone's coming."

Jack followed his glance. A sturdy woman of about fifty was hiking toward them. She looked experienced: high-laced boots, loose shirt and shorts, small backpack, and binoculars around her neck. She recognized their uniforms.

"You boys out practicing?" She chuckled. "I'm not lost!"

"No, ma'am," Jack said seriously. "We're looking for a little boy."

"Oh dear," she said. "How old?"

"Three and a half, about so high, with red hair. Where did you come in?"

"I took the Will Rogers Trail in from Topanga, and I haven't seen a soul. 'Course, I've mostly been looking for birds. But I certainly didn't see a little boy."

"How about adults?"

"I told you, not a soul."

"Okay." He glanced at Vince. "Thanks. Let somebody know if you see anything."

"Of course," she replied. "Good luck!"

3:53 P.M.

Bill Donner popped open a can of Coke and took a swallow, then wiped his hand across his bushy mustache. From his fire tower he could see most of the park's northwest corner. The radiophone beside him buzzed, and he picked it up.

"Donner."

"Bill, this is Pete. Any news?"

"Negative so far. Team four called in. They met a lady hiker up on Chicken Ridge. She'd come in from Topanga, but she didn't see anything."

Pete spoke wearily: "Okay. I talked to Jeff and they're sending out the choppers, should be up any minute."

Bill grunted. "Won't see much this time of year."

"I know, but—"

"Yeah. Keep in touch."

5:17 P.M.

Chris Jensen maneuvered the jeep slowly along the

firebreak while Bob Weiss scanned the hillside on both sides of the road.

"Hold it, Chris—looks like something crashed through on this side."

They got out and looked down the steep incline. The chaparral was broken in an indistinct path below the ridge. Bob got the rope and secured one end to the jeep's front bumper. Paying it out behind him, he started down the hillside.

"A little farther right!" Chris called. "Yeah, that's it."

Bob soon vanished in the thick growth. Chris heard branches cracking below, then Bob reappeared, using the rope to climb the steepest sections.

Chris leaned down to pull Bob up on the trail.

"Dead deer," Bob said briefly, coiling the rope. He wrinkled his nose in distaste. "Something's been chewing on it."

They climbed back into the jeep and continued slowly along the break.

6:48 P.M.

Ray Goodman and Bruce Bennett walked through the shallow ravine, systematically scanning the ground as they went.

"Getting dark."

"Yeah," Bruce replied. "We'll get the searchlights as soon as we get back down to the station."

"Mm. Wonder if they found him yet."

Bruce stopped, peering into the middle of a dense thicket. "Hey, Ray? Look at this."

They parted the bushes carefully, and Bruce pulled out a small blue-and-white object   a child's sneaker.

"Must belong to that kid   it hasn't been here long."

"I'll tie a marker, then let's get down and report it."
Ray attached a yellow marker strip to the chaparral and they hurried down the ravine toward the ranger station.

7:10 P.M.

It was nearly dark, and the ranch house kitchen was full of shadows. The Equestrian Patrol teams had clopped past the windows on their way back to the stables. Matt stood and turned on a light.

"Vicky?"

She sat staring straight ahead, her face a mask of despair. She hadn't cried at all yet, and he was starting to worry.

"Vicky?" He touched her shoulder. "I'm just going to see if they've heard anything. I'll be right back."

She looked at him without expression, and then stared again into space. Matt wasn't sure she had understood his words. With a worried frown, he went outside.

Seven or eight rangers stood crowded around the map in the ranger station. Pete looked around as Matt entered.

"Oh, good. Take a look at this, would you?" He pointed to the little sneaker on his desk.

"That's Ben's!" Matt said excitedly. "Where'd you find it?"

Pete held up one hand. "You're sure?" Matt nodded. "Well, don't get too optimistic. That's all we've found so far. We were just working out where we'll concentrate now. They'll be going out on foot with searchlights. If I were you, I'd try to get Mrs. Hunter to go home. It could be a long night."

Matt shook his head. "She won't go."

"I know." Pete rubbed the back of his neck wearily. "Well, anyway, I wouldn't tell her about this till we know what it means." He glanced at his watch. "That kid's been out there a long time. No use getting her hopes up."

As Matt returned to the ranch house, the search teams started out again, their sealed-beam searchlights playing across the ground in front of them.

9:13 P.M.

The weary search teams plowed through undergrowth and splashed across the infrequent streams, their lights casting weird shadows around them. Bob and Chris had worked their way up most of Rustic Canyon, and now they could hear two other search teams talking in low voices. Sound carried erratically on the mountains, and both men had long ago trained themselves to make allowances for it.

Suddenly Bob stopped in his tracks and touched Chris on the arm to silence him. Then both of them heard it—a feeble whimpering sound.

"Where the hell is it coming from?" Bob flashed his beam across the ravine on their right.

"I don't know, but it could be him," Chris answered as his light ricocheted off some low trees. "Let's try over here."

The men edged along the top of the ravine, shining their lights into its depths. Once a pair of bright eyes gleamed in the beam, and then they heard a large animal crashing through the underbrush.

"No way to get down here," said Bob. "No, wait a minute. I think there's some sort of trail up at the end of the canyon." They both stumbled across the rocky terrain, watching for the way down. In a few moments, Bob found the deer trail.

"Stay up here in case I break my neck or something. I'm going to see what's down there."

Cautiously he worked his way down to the bottom of the ravine and edged alongside the dribbling stream. He played his light from side to side, aware of what could jump out at him at any time. Then he heard the sound again. From there, it was easy to tell where it came from. He plunged ahead now, heedless of the thousands of tiny branches tearing at his jacket and pants.

The heavy searchlight picked up the child's figure just under the overhanging rock. He was lying curled up like a baby, his fists over his eyes. A couple of feet in front of him lay the stiff body of a fluffy puppy.

"I've got him!" Bob shouted. He ran to Ben and gathered him up in his arms. The child was still whimpering, and his little body felt cold.

Chris came crashing down, guided by Bob's light. He raced to the rocks. He saw Bob holding the child, whose little arms were clutched around the man's neck. Chris ripped off his jacket and tucked it around the terrified boy. Then he looked on the ground.

"Oh Christ," he groaned. He picked up the puppy's body and dropped a marker. Then he followed Bob as he climbed back up to the top.

It was a tired but jubilant group of men who tramped down toward the ranger hut. Bob was in the lead, still carrying Ben. It had been quicker to walk than to climb up to a trail and find a jeep. Several times the other men had tried to relieve Bob of the child's weight, but each time Bob started to transfer him, Ben's arms locked tighter, determined never to let go.

As they reached the open ground near the ranger station, a couple of the men broke out in a yell and one of them ran up ahead. Pete came out into the floodlit area in time to see the weary band approach.

Matt heard the commotion. He stole a glance at Vicky. She was still sitting quietly, her hands folded in her lap. God, I hope it's good news, he thought. He ran out of the ranch house and up toward the ranger's hut.

He could almost make out Ben as the lump Bob was carrying under Chris's jacket. He raced forward, stumbling over the uneven ground. "Is he all right?" he yelled to the men, and their happy grins told him before he could hear their response.

"Vicky!" Matt hollered. "They've found Ben!"

She came flying out of the ranch house and up the hill almost before Matt could move. Tears streamed down her face as she ran forward, her arms outstretched.

Vicky was sobbing by the time she reached the search teams standing near the ranger hut. "Ben! Oh, Ben!" she cried.

The child's eyes flickered. "Mom?" he croaked.

Chapter 8

The hospital corridor was quiet and almost empty. Halfway down toward the elevators, the nurses' station was brightly lit and two nurses leaned on the high counter, gossiping.

Matt held Vicky's hand in both of his own. Their faces were drawn and gray, showing the effects of the long night. "Come on," Matt urged. "The doctor said Ben's fine. He's just keeping Ben here for observation and to get some liquids into his system."

Vicky looked at him. "I know," she said. Then she stared again at the wall in front of them.

"There isn't anything you can do—certainly not until morning. Why don't you come back to the house and get some sleep?"

Vicky shook her head. "No, Matt. I know you mean well, and you're probably right. But I can't leave.

They've put a cot in Ben's room for me, so if I feel like I can actually sleep, I'll have that."

"But—" Matt tried to interrupt, but Vicky kept right on like a wind-up toy that, once it was started, couldn't be shut off.

"If I were home, I'd simply pace around and wish I were here. Besides, he might wake up, and then I'll definitely want to be here to let him know everything's okay."

Matt grinned tiredly, holding up his hand. "Okay, okay. I know when I'm beaten."

Vicky reached up and pushed back a stray lock of hair from his forehead. "You go on back. There's no sense in both of us being exhausted. And I'll feel better knowing you're in the house."

"Right, I make a great guard dog."

"Go on," she said, and she started walking him toward the elevator.

Once Matt was gone, Vicky paced around the corridor. Then she walked quickly down the stairs to the coffee machine on the floor below. She carefully carried the cardboard cup of steaming, muddy liquid back up to Ben's floor. The earnest young resident who was taking care of Ben stood at the nurses' station. Vicky headed toward him.

"Mrs. Hunter," he said, picking up a chart from the top of the counter. "I've got the blood-test results, and I'm sorry to say that they don't tell us much." He saw Vicky's face change from anticipation to disappointment. "Well, it's not too surprising. After all, it had been more than twelve hours from the time he was reported missing until we took the tests. There are a number of short-acting sedatives that would show no trace by now."

"That's all right, doctor," Vicky said, realizing that he was trying to be helpful. "I was just hoping... well, it doesn't matter. As long as Ben's okay."

"Oh, yes," he said, happy to be able to give her some positive news. "He's looking fine. I think you can take him home tomorrow afternoon." He looked at his watch and gave a little laugh. "I guess I mean *this* afternoon."

"Fine." Vicky smiled at him wanly and then turned down the corridor toward the little lounge.

She sat down heavily on the vinyl couch, and set her coffee on the plastic-topped table. Thank God Ben is all right, she thought for the thousandth time. I never want to have to live through something like that again.

She leaned back against the couch's unyielding surface. It was too bad the blood test hadn't shown any sign of a sedative in Ben's system. She could understand why the doctors had been skeptical—it *was* much more likely that a little boy had simply wandered away and gotten lost. And Ben's story of meeting the man with the puppy dog and then suddenly waking up in the dark under a rock was a little hard to believe. She would have found it hard to swallow herself, if it hadn't been the climax of his series of narrow escapes.

In fact, she reflected ruefully, I didn't know whether to believe Ben when he told me a man had opened our front gate, that day when I found him chasing his tricycle down West Channel. I can't blame the police for doubting that someone deliberately took him to the pool at the empty house. It's hard to know how much a three-and-a-half-year-old understands.

Sharp voices in the corridor drew Vicky's attention. Through the open lounge door she could see an older woman speaking to a younger one.

"I told you, you gotta watch them every second. I told you. And I told that husband of yours. Not that he ever listens to anything I say."

The younger woman sighed. "I know, Mama. But the children were all playing together in the sand. It wasn't Lester's fault."

"There ain't much that isn't his fault, if you ask me. If your pa and I didn't watch over you every second..."

The young woman glanced into the lounge and saw Vicky watching them. "Please, Mama," she said in a deliberately lowered voice.

"It's a wonder my beautiful grandchild ain't blinded. What kind of kids you let her play with anyway? Probably Lester's choosing."

Leading her mother away by the arm, the girl's voice trailed down the corridor. "You're probably right, Mama."

Vicky shook her head in amazement. There was a marriage in big trouble. Or maybe it was a sign of strength that it had been able to withstand pressure long enough for them to have a little girl old enough to play in the sand.

Getting up to stretch, Vicky walked the circuit of the small room and then sank back down onto the couch. Her thoughts returned to her own small son. She felt sure that a man *had* lured Ben away with a puppy as bait, and had then drugged him and carried him into the wilderness. But it was a pretty wild story. And without any evidence of the drug in his bloodstream, she had nothing concrete to tell the police.

But there had undoubtedly been a puppy.

Vicky thought back over the past couple of weeks, trying to make sense of what had happened. It had begun with the phone calls. They'd been more annoying than frightening, but now she thought of them as the beginning of this bizarre campaign of terror.

And of course there had been the fake call from the modeling agency—that was really the first clue that the whole thing somehow involved Ben.

She was convinced, now, that Ben was the focus of whatever was going on. Someone had tried to make it easy for him to get run over; it was so likely that a little boy on a trike would end up in the street. Then that terrifying evening when the man in the green station wagon had tried to crash her car—they'd waited until Ben was with her to do that. And after that, they'd taken Ben to the deserted house and left him alone by the pool. It was pure luck that Matt had found him before the inevitable drowning.

Vicky rubbed her forehead wearily and drank the lukewarm coffee. When they'd gone to Rosarito Beach, she'd been sure the Mexican man was following them, but nothing had really happened. Except—she frowned, trying to see a pattern—that night when they'd returned, the house had been burglarized and Tom's picture stolen.

How did that fit in with the attacks on Ben? The next day, Mrs. Garfield had been hit by a car that was surely aiming for Ben. And then, as if they were getting desperate, the most serious attempt of all: abandoning a small child in the depths of the mountain backcountry.

Why did anyone want to hurt Ben? Vicky walked to the grimy window and stood looking out at the lights of the city. What possible reason could there be to pursue a little boy? It wasn't as if he were the heir to the Rockefeller fortune. Could he possibly have seen something—some evidence of a crime or a shameful secret—that would be worth killing him for to keep him quiet? But that was absurd. If he'd seen something strange, he'd have told about it long before now, and anyway, what could a child his age understand that would make him dangerous?

There's nothing special about Ben except to me, she thought. He's just an ordinary little boy. It must be a psychopath, and that's why it doesn't make sense in a rational way. Maybe some psychotic killer has a phobia about red hair. But you'd think he'd give up after the first few attempts; there must be plenty of other redheads who would turn out to be easier to kill.

She frowned again and paced across the room. The psychopath theory wouldn't hold up, unless there were at least two of them working together. It was clear that there was more than one person involved. If the Mexican had been part of the plot, someone else had to be robbing the house while they were away. And the man in Will Rogers Park couldn't have been the same one who had taken Ben to the house with the pool. Ben would have recognized him, and Vicky felt certain that he wouldn't even have talked to him. She had made it very clear to Ben that he must never have anything to do with that man again. So there had to be at least two.

There was another reason why it couldn't be a psychopath. Now that Vicky thought about it, they'd been very careful *not* to kill Ben directly—they'd tried to set everything up for a fatal accident. A determined killer would have had plenty of opportunity to kill a little boy; his neck could have been broken as easily as that puppy's.

Vicky shuddered at the gruesome possibilities that flashed through her mind. She shook her head. They must have been trying to arrange an "accident." But why? She stopped short—maybe she was on the wrong track altogether. Maybe they were trying to get at her, *through* Ben. Could someone be trying to drive her away from her home or her job?

That's absurd, she thought tiredly. If someone wants the house, they could buy it—I've hardly been holding off developers with a shotgun. And anyone who wants my job can have it; God knows, it doesn't pay that well. Those cops asked about my boyfriends—but I'm not on bad terms with anyone. This whole vendetta is too desperate and too serious, and there is nothing in my normal life to account for it.

She turned back to the window and stared out unseeingly.

—The only thing that doesn't fit in is the photo of Tom. Does all this have something to do with him? It's the only thing I haven't thought about. But I can't believe that. Tom's life was as ordinary as mine, except for his tragic death. Perhaps they took the photo so they could recognize Ben. But no—there were pictures of Ben in the desk; they would have found them. And they'd already tried to kill Ben. I got those photos out to show the police.

Vicky rubbed her eyes.

—I'm exhausted—I'm just going around in circles. I can't make any sense of anything at this point.

She walked down the quiet corridor to Ben's room. The little night light beside his bed cast a faint illumination on his peaceful face. As she lay down on the cot next to him, she thought, he doesn't even look much like Tom.

Vicky slept fitfully, waking several times during the short night. Ben thrashed uneasily in his sleep, and

Vicky pulled up his covers and felt his damp forehead. But he didn't seem feverish and was sleeping soundly, so she lay down again and dozed off.

At about six-thirty, she heard him. "Mommy?" She woke immediately. Ben was sitting up, clutching the side rail of his hospital bed and staring at her in confusion.

"Hello, sweetie, how do you feel?" She went swiftly to his side and bent to kiss him.

"I need to pee."

Vicky lifted him down and walked with him to the bathroom. When they came back she sat on her cot and held Ben on her lap.

"Am I in the hospital?" he asked, looking around the room with interest.

"Yes, honey."

"Am I sick?"

Vicky wasn't sure how much he remembered of yesterday's ordeal. "No, not really," she said slowly. "But you were lost for a pretty long time yesterday, and the doctors wanted to make sure you were okay."

Ben looked puzzled. "How did I get lost?"

She struggled to find an answer that wouldn't be too frightening. "While you were talking to the man in the woods, you fell asleep," she said, watching his face. "He carried you through the woods. When you woke up, it was dark and you were lost. We looked for you for a long time, and then we found you."

"Was the man lost too?"

"I guess so." She wasn't sure this was the right way to handle it, but Ben seemed satisfied. He was quiet for a few moments, then he spoke tentatively.

"Mom, Dusty wouldn't wake up. I tried to wake him up, but he wouldn't."

Oh no, she thought. "I know, honey. Dusty fell down and got hurt. He was just a little baby dog."

"Did he get dead?"

"Yes, he did, Ben. I'm sorry."

He looked solemnly at her, but before he could say anything more, the door opened. A cheerful-looking nurse came in.

"Hello, Ben. How do you feel this morning?"

"Fine."

"How about hopping back up into your bed? I'm going to put the back up so it's like a big chair." She began turning the crank at the foot of the bed, and Ben watched in amazement as the head of the bed slowly rose. "Then I'm going to bring you some breakfast, and you can eat it on this little table. See, it swings right over your bed."

Ben was happy to go along with this idea. He was fascinated by all the equipment, and sat swiveling the bed tray on its pedestal. The nurse returned with his breakfast and he began investigating its contents, taking the cap off the juice cup and opening the little packet of plastic silverware.

"I'm sorry I don't have any breakfast for you, Mrs. Hunter, but I could get you some cofffe."

"Oh, no, thanks, I'll get something later on." Vicky helped Ben open the little box of cereal and pour milk over it in the dish.

He ate eagerly, and Vicky suddenly realized that he hadn't had anything to eat since the picnic lunch the day before. She buttered the blueberry muffin for him and watched indulgently as he consumed it, dropping crumbs all over the sheets.

"Good morning, I'm Dr. Levine." Vicky looked up to see a pleasant-faced young woman. "This must be

Ben. When you finish up that milk, I'm going to listen to your chest."

She took out her stethoscope and asked him to cough, listening carefully to his chest and back. She felt the glands below his ears and under his arms. "Do you hurt anywhere, Ben?"

"Uh-uh."

"Okay, turn your head to the side. And now the other way. Does that hurt?"

"Nope."

"Good. Now I'm going to look in your eyes. Look straight at that picture on the wall." She flicked on her ophthalmoscope and peered into his eyes.

She clicked off the light and smiled reassuringly at Vicky. "Looks to me as though this young man is fine. I think he ought to stay here until after lunch—he still looks a little pale and tired. I'd like him to stay in bed most of the morning, but you can take him home early this afternoon. That will be enough excitement for today."

"Should I keep him in for the rest of the week?"

"Oh no, that's not necessary. He may be a little more tired than usual, and he might want to nap during the day, but you don't have to restrict his activity. It's better to let him go back to his normal routine as soon as possible."

"What about all these scratches on his arms?" Vicky pointed to the angry-looking welts criss-crossing Ben's forearms and the backs of his hands where the sharp twigs in the underbrush had snapped back against his limp body.

"They all look perfectly clean—there doesn't seem to be any infection. I'm sure they'll be gone in a few days." Dr. Levine smiled at Ben and held out her hand. "Goodbye, Ben, I'm glad to have met you."

Ben shook her hand seriously. "Goodbye."

At the door, Dr. Levine looked back. "Don't worry, Mrs. Hunter. He'll bounce back quicker than you think."

After a while, the nurse reappeared with a pile of clean linen for the bed. Vicky asked her if Ben could have a bath. He soaked in the warm water and Vicky carefully washed his scratched arms, then tucked him back into bed. The nurse brought some books from the dayroom, and Vicky read him two or three stories. As she closed the book, she saw his eyelids drooping, and in a few minutes he was sound asleep again.

The door opened and Vicky looked around, her finger to her lips. Matt tiptoed in and stood beside her.

"He just fell asleep again," she said quietly.

Matt produced a package wrapped in bright paper. "I'll leave this here; he can open it when he wakes up." He handed Vicky a paper bag. "I hope those are okay. I found his underwear and some pants and a T-shirt in his dresser."

"Oh, Matt, thanks—I hadn't even thought about that."

"Come on," he whispered, "I bet you haven't eaten anything. Let's go and get some breakfast."

They stopped at the nurses' station and Vicky told them she'd be downstairs in the cafeteria if Ben woke up and wanted her. "Don't worry about a thing, Mrs. Hunter. We'll keep an eye on him. He sure is a cute one, with all that red hair. Bet he'll be quite a ladykiller when he gets older."

Matt steered Vicky to a table in the corner. They set

down their trays. "Now eat that before it gets too cold, Vicky. You must be famished by this time."

"I am a little hungry," she admitted.

"Good." He watched her approvingly. "What did the doctor say? How's Ben holding up after his ordeal?"

"I can take him home this afternoon. He seems to have recovered beautifully." She tried a laugh that fell short. Suddenly the polite conversation was too much for her. "Oh, Matt, I sat around last night and thought and thought. It's all so crazy. And I feel so helpless. No matter how I try to put the pieces together, I just end up going around in circles."

Matt put down his coffee cup slowly. "I've been doing a lot of thinking myself, Vicky," he said at last. "There's something I have to tell you." He took a deep breath. All night, he'd wondered how he could say what he now felt he must, without hurting her. He had already envisioned her shock, and maybe even anger, when he started destroying the little security she had left. But he couldn't keep it a secret any longer.

"Tom's name wasn't really Tom Hunter. His name was Lloyd Thomas Whitney."

Vicky looked at him in bewilderment. "What do you mean?"

"Remember that TV newscast about the real estate tycoon who just died? Your husband was his oldest son."

"But that's not possible." Vicky shook her head in disbelief.

"It's true, Vicky. When we were in college together, he was Lloyd Whitney, my rich roommate. But he never liked the way his father made all those millions; he thought it was dirty money. He didn't want any part of it, or of his family. So after graduation, he legally changed his name and dropped out of sight. I was the only one he told, and I've kept it a secret because he asked me to." Matt pulled a sheet of paper out of his pocket. "This is the court order changing his name to Tom Hunter. You can see there's no doubt about his original name either." He handed the official-looking form across the table.

Vicky took it and looked at it briefly. Matt was right. Both names appeared in the document along with the judge's signature and the state seal at the bottom. Vicky faced Matt, but her eyes looked inward. "How could he not have told me? We were married. I was his wife."

Matt sat across from her in silence, watching the pain cloud her eyes. "I can hardly believe it," she said as if talking to herself. "He was lying to me all the time, about his whole life." She glanced down at the court order again. "Lloyd Whitney." Then she raised her eyes to Matt's. "Where did you get this?"

Matt looked down into his coffee cup. In a low voice, he said, "Remember when you told me there was an envelope full of Tom's papers that you'd never opened?"

"You looked through my desk?" Vicky's eyes flashed. "When was this?"

Still refusing to meet her accusing stare, he said, "I know it sounds terrible, and I don't blame you for being angry. But I hoped you would never have to know." At last he raised his eyes to her face. "It was obvious that the name Whitney meant nothing to you, and I realized that Tom had never told you. I knew that paper existed, and I wanted to spare you the pain of discovering it someday without any preparation." He paused, but Vicky made no response. "I thought that if

Tom hadn't wanted you to know, it wasn't up to me to change that. I felt I was respecting his decision."

"But how could you keep something like that a secret?" Her cheeks were flushed with angry color. "First Tom, and now you—you've treated me like a child who can't be trusted with the truth."

"I'm sorry, Vicky. I thought I was doing the right thing."

There was a short silence. Then Vicky said bitingly, "And now you've changed your mind. Am I allowed to ask why you decided to tell me now?"

"I think the Whitneys must be the cause of the attacks on Ben," he replied bluntly. "The whole thing began just about the time Lloyd Whitney died."

Vicky's eyes widened. "It's just hit me—he was Ben's grandfather."

Matt nodded. Her face suddenly paled. "My God, don't you remember—oh no, I heard it on the way to work—they're looking for his oldest son. He left his company to Tom! But they don't know Tom is dead."

"I think they do," Matt said somberly. "Or at least someone does. The old man must have left his estate to Tom and Tom's children. That means someone is trying to get rid of Ben before the lawyers find out about him. And don't you see, Vicky, that's why it's all been made to look like accidents. They didn't want any investigation that might lead to the discovery of Ben's relationship to the Whitneys."

Vicky hugged herself and shivered. "You must be right—it's the only thing that makes sense. And I think I know who it is. On the radio they said that Charles Whitney was running the business now, and he's the only other person involved." She paused and stared at Matt. "But how could anyone try to kill his own nephew? It's so ugly." She shuddered, and Matt reached out to put his hand over hers. "It must be him," she went on. "The radio broadcast said he was going to contest the will and try to have his brother declared legally dead."

Still holding her hand, Matt said slowly, "Vicky, how *did* Tom die?"

"It was a freak accident. He was on location in Arizona. They were shooting that film *Dusty Death* down there. Anyway, they'd finished shooting for the day and he was taking a shower in his motel room. He had taken the radio into the bathroom with him, and somehow it fell into the tub. That's where they found him. He was electrocuted." She saw Matt's look of mounting disbelief and went on apologetically, "I know it sounds like a dumb thing to do. He must have been tired and just not thinking. But who ever thinks those bizarre accidents will happen to them?"

Matt was staring at her incredulously. "Vicky, that's not possible."

"Well, the police—" she began.

"No, no, you don't understand," Matt went right on. "Tom couldn't have done something like that. He was a total fanatic about electrical stuff near any kind of plumbing. His cousin or his uncle or someone died in the same kind of accident when Tom was a kid, and it made a big impression on him. I remember when we were rooming together, the light fixture in our bathroom gave out and I decided to move a table lamp in there. Tom went crazy and gave me a whole lecture on how dangerous it was." He shook his head. "There's no way Tom could have taken a radio into a bathroom, especially in a motel where there's no room to turn around. I just don't believe it."

"I can't help it, Matt, that's what happened."

Matt stared at Vicky without really seeing her, tapping a spoon absently on the table. Finally he said, "I'm not so sure." His fingers spread to ward off Vicky's beginning of a protest. "Just think about it for a minute. What if it wasn't an accident."

"Oh, no."

But Matt went on, his low, reasonable voice trying to mitigate Vicky's anxiety, while forcing her to explore this new and dreadful possibility. "What if Charles Whitney's attempt to inherit his father's millions started much earlier than we've thought?"

Her eyes widening in horror, she whispered, "Are you saying that Charles Whitney killed his own brother? Just for money? I can't imagine how anyone could be such a monster."

"Of course, I can't be certain. I don't know how Charles could have found Tom. But if that's what happened, it explains an awful lot. I just don't believe Tom's death was accidental—at least, not that kind of accident. But it wouldn't have been hard to make it look that way."

Vicky nodded unwillingly. "But that was two years ago. Why would he try to kill Ben now?"

"He probably thought that if Tom weren't around, he'd inherit the money himself. He wouldn't have known about his father's will until just recently, when the old man died. And if he had already tracked Tom down, it would be easy to find you and Ben."

Vicky looked at him in protest. "But I didn't even know Ben had any connection with the Whitneys."

Matt shook his head. "Charles couldn't have known that. He's probably been expecting you to make your claim at any moment. But even if he thought you didn't know, he couldn't take the chance that you'd ever find out. Ben is a walking time bomb to Charles Whitney."

It took her a few moments to absorb the dreadful logic of Matt's argument. "That's horrible," she said at last. "No wonder Tom wanted nothing to do with his family. He must have had such an unhappy time of growing up."

"He did."

She went on more slowly, "That must be why he never told me. He couldn't bear to drag all that ugliness into the new life he had created for himself." Vicky shook her head sadly. "Poor Tom. It must have been so hard." She looked at Matt with mingled pain and appeal. "I think he would have told me eventually."

Again he covered her hand with his and said sympathetically, "I'm sure he would." After a moment he continued, "The question is, what do we do now? We don't have any proof of all this—I'm afraid it won't be easy to convince the police."

Vicky looked surprised. "But Matt, now that I know what's going on, there's no problem. I don't want the money. I didn't marry Lloyd Whitney; he was already Tom Hunter when I met him. The Whitney family had no part in our life together, and they have no part in my life now. Besides, I wouldn't go near those people or their money—it makes my skin crawl to think about it." She finished the last of her coffee and pushed back her chair. "I'm going to call Charles Whitney right now and tell him Ben and I don't want any part of the Whitney money."

"I don't think it will be that easy," Matt said cautiously.

"Well, they can work out the details later. The important thing is to tell him so he'll leave us alone." She stood up. "How do you think he's listed?"

Matt watched through the glass doors of the phone booth as Vicky got the number from Information and dialed the call. She fed change into the slots, and then talked for a while. When she hung up, she opened the door slowly, her face disappointed.

"He's out of town until tomorrow," she reported. "I talked to his secretary. She didn't even seem interested in taking my name." Vicky suppressed a sigh. "So I guess I'll have to call again in the morning."

Matt put his arms around her shoulders. "I was thinking about it while you were on the phone. I'm afraid it isn't a matter of a simple phone call. If we're right about Charles Whitney, he won't accept a call from you. I think the only way to handle this is in person. I'll fly to Arizona in the morning and see him myself. That way he'll know that someone besides you is aware of what's going on and he'll be afraid to try anything else. He won't refuse to see me; Tom's court order changing his name will be a fine letter of introduction." He looked down at her. "Whatever happens in the end about the money, at least Ben will be safe."

"That's a good idea. But Matt, I think I should go and see him myself. You've been wonderful, but I can't ask you to solve all my problems for me."

"What would you do with Ben while you're gone? No, Vicky, you stay here and I'll go to Arizona and see him. It's only an hour by plane—I'll be back tomorrow evening."

"I guess you're right," she said slowly. "Thanks, Matt. I really appreciate your taking so much trouble for us." She smiled up at him. "Just tell him we aren't interested in the money."

Matt nodded. "Right. Now let's see how that son of yours is doing."

Chapter 9

"Do you want another drumstick, Ben?"

Ben paid no attention. His eyes were glued to the rerun of 'Wild Kingdom.' "Look, Mom, baby penguins! They're going swimming!"

"Yes, aren't they funny?" Vicky bent to put more chicken on his plate on the floor. "How about you, Matt?"

"Sure, it's delicious."

Vicky sat down with a little sigh. "It's nice to be sitting here eating dinner in front of the TV like normal people." She laughed. "I don't usually let Ben do this, but I'm so happy he's home from the hospital that I wanted to give him a treat. This is his favorite show."

They watched in silence for a while, enjoying both the show and Ben's rapt response to it. When the commercial came on, Ben stood up.

"Mom, here's how penguins walk." He waddled

around the room, his toes turned out as far as they could go, and his face solemn.

Matt laughed. "All you need is a white tie and tails, and you'd fit right in down there in the Antarctic."

"Matt, how come penguins don't get cold?"

"They're used to all that snow and ice, Ben. They have oil on their feathers, and that keeps the water off their skin. Their feathers keep them warm, like a parka keeps you warm in cold weather."

Ben nodded. "That's neat."

Another commercial came on, this one for life insurance, and Vicky said, "I saw Mrs. Garfield today, Ben, while you were sleeping at the hospital. She asked me to say hello to you."

"How long does she get to stay in the hospital, Mom?"

"Maybe for another week or two, honey, and she'll have to stay home for a while after that."

"Does she have one of those neat tables to eat in bed like I had?"

"Sure." Vicky smiled. "When she comes home, we can pick some flowers and take them to her at her house."

"Okay." Marlin Perkins was back, this time with walruses, and Ben's attention was once more focused on the TV.

Vicky leaned back. "Matt, I can't tell you how relieved I am to finally know what's been going on. I felt like I was going insane—I couldn't understand *why*. Now that I know what they want, I feel I can deal with it." She made a face. "Although, of course, you're really the one who's going to deal with it. I still feel guilty about letting you do that."

Matt put a finger on her lips. "No more of that; I'll

be as relieved as you are to have this thing finished. It's been a nightmare for all of us."

When the show was over and Ben was in bed, Vicky returned to the living room. Matt went on as though there had been no interruption. "How much do you think Ben understands of all this? He's such a happy, outgoing kid, I'd hate to think that he'd end up all insecure and scared."

"I worry about that too. He hasn't talked about any of his bad experiences. Being in the hospital was a big adventure, but he hasn't said a word about what went on before. He doesn't seem to be having nightmares or bad dreams, at least. Anyway, I really don't know what he knows or how much he understands. And I can't ask him about it or push him to talk to me. If he's not scared, I certainly don't want to make him that way by making a big deal out of it."

"I see what you mean. It's hard to know what these little kids are thinking," he said.

Vicky rested her head on his shoulder. "I'll be so glad when this is really over and I can live my own life again."

"So will I." He kissed the tip of her nose lightly, then said, "I've got to get up early to catch a plane."

In the morning, Ben tagged after Matt as he shaved and found a presentable shirt and tie. He watched in awe as Matt tied his necktie and then, swearing, pulled it loose and started over. Ben walked out to the kitchen.

"Mom, Matt's getting dressed up."

"Yes, I know. He's going to an important meeting today."

"Mom?"

"Yes, honey?"

"Matt said a bad word. He said 'shit.'"

Vicky suppressed a smile. "Well, I guess he's in a hurry. It's not a good thing to say, though. How about sitting down and having some Rice Krispies?"

Matt rushed in and poured himself some coffee. "I've got to run. The traffic's going to be murder down to the airport."

Vicky handed him a slice of toast. "You won't get anything to eat on the plane." She looked at him with approval. "I've never seen you wear a tie before. You look ready to take on big business."

"That's the idea." He grinned and put down his cup. Rumpling Ben's hair, he said, "See you later, tiger."

Vicky walked outside with him to the van. "Be careful, Matt, and good luck."

"Thanks." He bent to kiss her swiftly, and then swung into the van.

"Let me know what happens."

"I will." He backed down the driveway and drove off.

Over the last of his Rice Krispies, Ben looked at Vicky. "Mom, who was that man at the park?"

"I don't know, honey," she answered slowly. A frown of concern clouded her face. Ben said nothing, and Vicky wondered how to go on.

"Mom?"

"Yes, Ben?"

"Am I going to school tomorrow?"

"Yes, I think you will. Don't you want to?"

"Yeah. But I don't want to go to that park." He sounded uncertain.

Vicky knelt beside his chair and held him close. "You don't have to go there, sweetie. Everything is going to be fine now."

The phone rang. Giving Ben another hug, Vicky went to answer it.

"Vicky? It's Paula."

"Oh, hi. I meant to call you earlier to let you know I won't be in today. Ben just got home from the hospital yesterday and I thought I'd hang around with him."

"Stay home? But today's our meeting with Jason Freeman. I called to remind you."

"Oh Christ! I totally forgot."

"You can make it, can't you?"

"Oh, Paula, my sitter's sick and I—" She heard the doorbell ring. "Look, Paula, someone's at the door. I'll call you back."

"Okay. But Vicky, we're counting on you. You know how bizarre that guy is."

"Yeah, sure. I'll do what I can. I've got to run. Talk to you later." She hung up the phone and saw Peter, with his long blond ponytail, standing in the doorway talking to Ben.

"Hi," she said. "Come on in."

He walked in and stood awkwardly in the middle of the room. "I saw your car, so I knew you were home," he explained shyly. "I just wanted to see how Ben was doing."

"Oh, that was sweet of you, Peter. He's fine, just a little tired still. Why don't you sit down? Would you like some coffee?"

"Yeah, thanks, if it's no trouble." He produced a small brown paper sack from behind his back. "I brought this for Ben—sorry it's not wrapped up."

"How nice! A surprise for Ben. Come on, honey, open it up. Let's see what it is."

Ben took the paper sack and tore it open eagerly. Inside was a square box. He opened the lid and pulled out a long coil of metal.

"A Slinky! I haven't seen one of those for ages. Peter, that's great." She turned to Ben, who was staring at the Slinky with baffled interest. "Maybe Peter will show you how it works."

She went to check on the coffee and returned to find Peter and Ben on the floor, building a set of steps with Ben's blocks. Peter sat back and said, "Okay, Ben, let's try it now."

The Slinky moved end-over-end down the steps, hesitantly at first, and then gathering speed. Ben clapped his hands in delight.

"It walked down the stairs! Let's do it again."

Concentrating carefully, he set it on the top step and pushed it gently to start another descent.

"Looks like the Slinky is a big success, Peter." Vicky smiled. "I'm glad you came by. I wanted to thank you again for taking care of Ben the other day. I'm lucky to have such a good neighbor."

"Oh, it was no trouble. I really enjoyed it. Actually, that's partly why I came over. I thought maybe I could stay with Ben in case you had some errands or shopping or something you had to do."

Vicky rescued her cup from the coffee table just as the Slinky was advancing upon it. "That's a tempting offer, Peter. As a matter of fact, there *is* something. I really should go in to my office for an hour or so. There's a lunch meeting that's been planned for some time. Could you possibly come for a couple of hours around lunchtime?"

He nodded. "Sure. The only thing is, I'd have to

leave at two. I have an appointment at two-forty-five, and I can't be late."

"That would work out fine. If I leave at noon, I can easily be home by two." She paused and looked at Ben.

"Honey, I'm going to go to my office later for a little while, and Peter's going to stay with you while I'm gone. Is that okay?"

Hardly glancing up from the Slinky, he said, "Sure, Mom."

She turned to Peter. "Are you sure this is all right? I don't like to impose on you, but it certainly would be a big help."

"Really, it's no problem. I'm happy to do it."

"Well, that's terrific. I'll just call my office and let them know that I can make it. Ben, why don't you get ready to go to the grocery store with me? We'll run over there and get something good for you and Peter to have for lunch." She opened the door for Peter. "Thanks again. I'll see you at noon."

She came back inside and dialed the office number. "Paula? It's Vicky. I've got a sitter, so I can come in for this meeting. But I have to leave by one-thirty at the latest."

"Oh good, that's great. I'm glad you worked that out. I wasn't looking forward to coping with Jason by myself."

"I know what you mean," Vicky said with a laugh. "But listen, I won't get there until twelve-thirty so we'd better go over what we're going to discuss with him now."

"Well, Jason's never going to get a green light on this project unless the script is drastically revised. But he's so high on this writer that he can't see the problems. You know how he is—the guy can't write his way out of a paper bag, but Jason thinks he's fabulous."

"I know," Vicky said with a sigh. "But I've been thinking about it. I think I see a way the script can be salvaged. It'll have to be more or less gutted—the whole middle section has to go. It's too bad Jason is so protective of this writer, because we'll have to slug our way through every page."

"That's why I need you here. We have to convince Jason to let us meet with the writer alone. That's the only way it'll get done. I think we've got to play the old good-guy-bad-guy game. I'm going to be very firm about the project not getting a go as it stands. And you're going to be sympathetic and eager to help Jason, and suggest that you and the writer can work it out together. Jason likes you anyway, so that'll help."

"Okay. Let's hope it works," Vicky said. "See you at twelve-thirty in the commissary."

Vicky put down the phone and called toward the bathroom, "Ben? Honey, let's move it. We've got to get to the market and back before noon."

Matt's plane touched down at the Phoenix airport, and a few moments later he was walking through the concourse. It emptied into a large square hall with the usual glass-fronted airport service shops on both sides. Matt glanced up to his left and stopped involuntarily, staring. An incredible mural ran all along the wall between the shop doors and the ceiling—a gigantic phoenix rising from its ashes in full, vibrant color. Matt was momentarily amazed that none of the other people scurrying toward planes or off to baggage-claim didn't give the impressive phoenix so much as a passing glance. Then he too hurried on through the hall and out toward the front of the airport and the waiting cabs.

Inside the airport, the influeunce of the Pueblo and Navajo Indians on the arts and fabrics of the region was quite apparent, but outside, from Matt's taxi, Phoenix looked much like any other city. A few glass-and-steel skyscrapers spired skyward out of the middle of downtown. Otherwise, the city appeared as flat as the desert on which it was built.

Since the airport was right on the edge of downtown Phoenix, the cab ride to the Whitney Building was a short one. A few odd-sounding street names reminded Matt of the original inhabitants of this land. The air was clear and the sky brilliant blue, but he was thankful to be inside the air-conditioned cab. Already the temperature was pushing a hundred degrees.

Matt paid the cab driver and stepped into the cool foyer of the Whitney Building. An old four-story stucco structure, it had been completely renovated inside. Matt's advertising background had given him a highly developed sense for what sells. He stopped and looked around in appreciation of the superb packaging. Hand-chipped slate-tile flooring was accented here and there with beautifully woven Indian rugs. Low-slung couches were covered in soft glove leather. Concealed spotlights in the ceiling cleverly lit the collection of Old West oils on the walls. A ten-foot barrel cactus stood in the corner, and a fabulous saguaro, with its tall, slender body and angular arms, created a background for the well-groomed, forty-year-old receptionist smiling at Matt. The fragrance of expensive perfume wafted toward him as he approached her desk.

"Good morning. May I help you?"

"Yes. I'm here to see Charles Whitney."

She kept smiling. "May I have your name? What time is your appointment?" Her gold Mark Cross pen was poised over her handsome leather logbook.

Matt smiled back. "My name is Matthew London, and I'm afraid I don't have an appointment."

She carefully placed her pen back on her desk, and her smile became regretful. "I'm sorry, sir. Mr. Whitney doesn't see anyone without an appointment."

Matt kept his smile pasted in place. In a voice loud enough to be heard by the elevator starter, he said, "Thank you very much." Then he strode to the bank of elevators and stepped inside the open car. There was only one floor Charles Harmon Whitney could possibly be on. "Four, please."

As Matt stepped out on the fourth floor, he noted that the same expensive decorator had been let loose with an even more generous budget. The whole floor seemed to be comprised entirely of an open reception area, a boardroom, and a large office with the shiny brass plaque on its door, naming the new company president. A striking brunette behind an enormous desk looked up at him. At Matt came closer, she sneezed, wiping her nose and smudging her careful eye makeup with a dainty handkerchief.

"Sorry. Isn't it the dumbest thing, having a cold in this kind of weather?"

"Bless you," said Matt.

"Thanks." She tucked her hankie into the sleeve of her fashionable but somewhat low-cut shirred-silk peasant blouse. "What can I do for you?"

"I'm here to see Mr. Whitney."

"Oh dear. I thought I canceled all his appointments

for today. He's still in L.A." She thumbed through the appointment book on her desk. "What was your name?"

"Still in L.A.? Gee, that's a shame. I really do need to see him. Where did you say he was staying?"

Belatedly cautious, she looked up at Matt, making it a thorough inspection. "I'm not allowed to give out that information. What did you say your name was?"

"Matthew London." He turned and pressed the elevator button. "You can tell Mr. Whitney I'll be in touch." As he entered the elevator, Matt saw the girl carefully noting his name, a puzzled expression on her face.

As the elevator doors closed, Matt's face became grim. Charles Whitney in Los Angeles—that meant that Ben was still in danger. Matt's long legs carried him out of the elevator, across the foyer, and through the doors to the street before the carefully coiffed blonde at the reception desk could utter a word.

Outside, Matt looked around. The new Hyatt Regency, with its revolving rooftop restaurant, was just a block away. That would be the best place to find a cab, and surely there would be pay phones in the lobby. He needed to get in touch with Vicky right away. Her mood this morning had been so lighthearted and exuberant—she had acted as though all their problems were solved. He had to tell her to sit tight and not to get careless now, not until he had actually spoken to Charles Whitney and had the assurance that all would be well.

Matt dropped a dime and a nickel into the pay phone, and dialed Vicky's number in L.A. He had a stack of coins in front of him, but he never had a chance to use them. Vicky's phone rang and rang without an answer. Finally Matt hung up. He could call from the airport. He went outside and hopped into the first cab in line. "Take me to the airport."

When he got there, Matt first checked on planes to L.A. The next one leaving stopped in San Diego on the way, but it would still get him to L.A. sooner than the next nonstop an hour later. The flight was already boarding as Matt dumped fifteen cents into a pay phone and tried Vicky again. While the phone rang, the last boarding announcement for Matt's flight came booming over the loudspeakers. He hung up and walked quickly to the gate.

In Los Angeles, Vicky, Peter, and Ben were outside as Vicky fished out her car keys and got into her car. When she heard the phone, she climbed out of the car again and ran to get it. But all she heard at the other end was a dial tone.

Vicky came back outside. "I hope that wasn't Matt," she said to Peter. "I really don't want to miss his call. I've left my office number on the pad on the desk. If he calls, be sure and tell him to call me there." She bent to kiss Ben. "'Bye, honey, have fun. Maybe you can take your Slinky out on the front steps after lunch." Turning to Peter, she went on, "I think Ben may be ready for a nap about one or one-thirty—he's still kind of exhausted. You could go in his room with him and read him a story before he goes to sleep. I'll be home before he wakes up, I'm sure." She got into the VW and started the engine. "'Bye, see you soon."

As her car disappeared around the corner, Peter turned to Ben. "Ready for lunch?"

"Yeah!"

They went into the kitchen and Ben said, "Guess what we're having for lunch."

"What?"

"Baloney-with-olives sandwiches and dill pickles! We went to the store and Mom let me choose what I wanted for lunch. I *love* baloney that has olives in it."

"Sounds pretty good." Peter opened the refrigerator and took out the sandwhiches Vicky had made.

"The pickles are in that jar," Ben reminded him.

"Okay." Peter took out the big glass jar. "Do you want some milk?"

"Uh-huh."

When Peter had assembled the lunch, he asked, "How about eating outside?"

"Yeah, a picnic!"

They went out the back door and sat on the grass. The inevitable ants appeared, and they both watched with interest as the ants carried away the breadcrumbs they had dropped. When the sandwiches were consumed, Peter said, "Got room for dessert? I happen to know that your Mom put a surprise in the freezer."

"She did?"

Peter went inside and returned with two dishes of frozen yogurt. Ben's eyes lit up.

"Oh boy, strawberry frogurt!"

Ben spooned it up with gusto, but by the time he had finished, his eyelids were beginning to droop. He went inside without protest and lay down on his bed. Soon, lulled by Peter's gentle reading, he was asleep.

In the employees' parking lot of 20th Century-Fox, a man lifted the engine cover of a red VW. The guard in the gate hut glanced without interest at the man with car trouble, and then turned to answer the phone.

The man bent over the engine and located the part he was looking for. He pulled a pair of pliers from his pocket and, with a quick wrench, yanked the part off. Stuffing it in his pocket, he walked off toward the back of the lot.

Jason Freeman held the door open and bowed extravagantly as Vicky and Paula walked out of the studio commissary. He clasped their elbows and steered them carefully down the three shallow steps to the sidewalk. Tall and slender, with thin, sandy hair and a drooping ginger mustache, Jason was the epitome of an effete Englishman.

On the sidewalk, he took Paula's hand in his long fingers. Turning her palm upward, he bent and kissed it. "As ever, my *dear* Paula, *such* a pleasure. And such a quaint retreat for an intimate luncheon. We must do it again *soon*."

He pivoted gracefully and placed his fingertips on Vicky's temples. Dropping a kiss on her forehead, he lowered his voice. "Vicky, darling girl, you are balm to a troubled spirit. I feel refreshed, renewed, at our every encounter. Yours to command, my sweet, always."

He stepped back and surveyed them both. Supressing a giggle, Vicky said, "Nice to see you, Jason. Just tell Alan to call me, and don't worry about a thing. We'll get it all straightened out."

He sketched a brief bow. *"Merci mille fois. Au revoir, mes cheries."*

They watched him move swiftly toward the low-slung car in the no-parking zone at the curb. It was a perfectly restored 1961 Morgan in British racing green, complete with hand-tufted leather upholstery, an oiled wooden steering wheel, and gleaming wire wheels. His spare figure, clad entirely in black—silk knit turtleneck fitted English twill trousers, and soft Italian leather boots—lowered itself smoothly into the car. With a rattling roar, the car leapt forward as Jason flung a hand above his head in farewell.

Vicky rolled her eyes at Paula. "Doesn't that guy ever sweat?" The two of them collapsed in helpless laughter.

In heavy English accents, Paula said, "Vicky, *darling* girl, *so* glad you could be here. It was—" But she couldn't go on, and they burst out in uncontrollable giggles again.

Finally Paula wiped the tears from her eyes. "God, let's not do that again very soon. I couldn't take it. What a madman!"

"Yes," Vicky responded. "This is glamorous Hollywood! But look on the bright side; maybe this film will take three years to complete, and by that time Jason will have a co-production deal with China or something."

"Well, anyway," Paula sighed, "I'm glad you were here. I'm not strong enough to deal with Jason by myself."

"Who is?" Vicky looked at her watch. "I've got to leave—it's twenty-five to two and I promised my sitter I'd be home by two o'clock. I'll call you tomorrow." She turned and began to walk away, then wheeled around. "Ta-ta, Paula, it's been *such* a pleasure." Still chuckling, she moved briskly toward the parking lot.

Vicky waved happily to the studio guard in his little hut at the back gate as she trotted down the hill to her car. It was still surrounded by the vehicles that had been there when she arrived; there was little traffic out of the employee parking lot during the middle of the day.

She slipped behind the wheel and stuck her key into the ignition. Turning the key, she pumped the accelerator, expecting to hear the midget roar of the engine. Instead, she heard nothing. She stared at the dash unbelievingly as she tried it again. Nothing. Drumming her fingers on the steering wheel, Vicky waited, hoping that whatever mysterious problem her usually trustworthy little car had would clear itself up. But when she turned the key for the third time, she got the same non-response. Shaking her head in annoyance, Vicky got out and opened the lid at the back of the VW and peered in. Everything seemed to be where it was supposed to be.

Who are you kidding? she thought. The only thing you'd notice was if the entire engine was missing. She slammed the lid down with a force that shook the little bug. Throwing open the door, she got in and tried to start it once more. There was nothing she could do. She looked helplessly at the guard shack and the back of the studio, dozens of yards away.

If she used the guard's telephone to call the Auto Club, it would take at least a half-hour for them to get there. And rounding up someone at the studio to walk all the way back down there and look at the car would just waste more time.

Vicky looked at her watch. It was almost ten to two. She had to get home. Grabbing her purse and keys, she lurched out of the car and headed for the Century Plaza Hotel, whose rear side loomed up on the hill on the far edge of the parking lot. It was a long uphill climb past the delivery docks and around to the front of the hotel, but at least she would be able to get a cab there.

Halfway up, Vicky's anger and frustration turned to panic. Was this another episode in the plot against Ben? Had someone deliberately sabotaged her car?

Don't be silly, she chided herself. Matt's already seen Charles Whitney and gotten everything straightened out.

Her watch moved relentlessly toward two o'clock as she panted up the hill in the hot sun. Would Peter leave Ben alone in the house when she didn't get back in time? He had sounded awfully definite about the appointment he had. If Ben was sleeping, Peter might easily leave. What would happen if Ben woke up to an empty house? She forced herself into a run as she reached Avenue of the Stars and turned into the hotel drive-through.

There was a cab sitting in front of the hotel entrance, in the center of the semi-circular drive. As Vicky raced along the sidewalk toward it, the taxi began to move. Two suited businessmen were sitting in the back seat. Damn, thought Vicky. The curb lane reserved for waiting cabs was empty. Quickly, she spotted the doorman and asked where the taxis were.

"Should be one along pretty soon," he said laconically.

"Can't you call one for me?" Vicky asked.

The doorman looked at her skeptically, then repeated, "There'll be some here shortly."

Defeated, Vicky stood in front of the long, glass-fronted lobby and waited. In Los Angeles, cab service was remarkably poor. The whole concept of hailing a cruising cab was totally foreign, and to call one by phone guaranteed at least a half-hour wait. If there were taxi stands, no one in Los Angeles had ever seen them. The only places where it was possible to find a cab were at the airport and in front of the major hotels. Vicky knew that there was nothing she could do but wait.

The big jet dropped low over the San Diego Freeway and floated onto the runway at LAX.

"Welcome to Los Angeles International Airport, where the local time is 2:03 P.M. Please remain in your seats, with your seatbelts fastened, until we have come to a complete stop at the gate and the captain has turned off the seatbelt sign. On behalf of the captain and crew, I would like to thank you for flying with us today, and wish you a pleasant stay in Los Angeles."

As always, almost everyone had jumped up into the aisles and started gathering briefcases, packages, and jackets before the plane was halfway to the gate. They lined up at the exit door and pushed eagerly onto the waiting jetway.

Matt walked down the escalator and through the long tunnel separating the plane gates from the street lobby. Thankfully passing the throng crowding hopefully around the baggage carousels, Matt strode out to the street and crossed to the parking lot. When he reached his van, he unlocked it, yanked off his jacket, and hopped in. He was in line for the pay booth before he remembered money, and grumbling to himself, he scrunched around until he could pull a couple of dollars out of his pocket. For some reason, everyone in front of him had to have a receipt for his parking money, each of which had to be written out by hand. Matt spent a couple of seconds mentally composing a letter to whoever ran these concessions. Then he realized that he should have tried to call Vicky once again while he was still in the airport. Oh, well, there wasn't anything he could do about it now, and it would be quicker to just keep driving once he got out of the airport area than to try and find a gas station pay phone. He gunned his accelerator angrily, willing the line to move along. Where had Vicky been when he'd tried to call earlier? he wondered. Maybe she had taken Ben to the park or something like that. He only hoped Whitney hadn't become so desperate that he'd make an outright attempt at killing them both.

Peter checked the clock on Vicky's stove once again—two-ten. He paced around the kitchen, peering out the window to see if the little red VW was pulling into the drive. It wasn't. He walked into the living room and looked out the window there. Where was she? He really couldn't be late for his appointment. Fortunately, he'd already loaded his portfolio of drawings and watercolors into his car. But he couldn't hang around here much longer. It would be disastrous to show up late for this long-awaited job interview. He was already cutting it close.

As he passed near the phone, he saw Vicky's office number. Quickly, wondering why he hadn't thought of it before, he dialed her number. The call was finally routed to Paula's office.

"Vicky? Oh no, she left at twenty-five to two. She should be home any minute. I know she was concerned about getting back before you had to leave."

"Oh, okay, thanks. Sounds like she'll be here right away."

He hung up and found a pad and pencil on the desk.

Dear Vicky,
   It's almost 2:15 and I have to leave. Your office said you were on your way home. Ben is sound asleep. Sorry, but it's important.

                                                Peter

He propped the note against a bowl on the kitchen table. Then he tiptoed into Ben's room and looked down at the sleeping boy. Ben was breathing slowly and evenly, obviously deeply asleep. Satisfied, Peter tiptoed out again and closed the door gently.

He went outside and looked along the street, hoping to see Vicky's VW. Then, with a worried glance at his watch, he pulled the front door shut and walked quickly toward his own car. He still felt uneasy at leaving Ben alone, but it was too late now to do anything else. Reaching his car, he got in and, with one more look down the obstinately empty street, drove off to his appointment.

At long last, a taxi drew up in front of the Century Plaza Hotel. Vicky rushed forward to claim it. The doorman followed at a more leisurely pace. He bent to help an elderly, expensively dressed woman lift her substantial weight out of the back seat. Inside the cab, her equally portly husband was trying to extract coins from his trousers pocket.

"Just a moment, driver, I'm sure I have some loose change," Vicky heard him say importantly.

The driver got out and stretched, then walked around to open the trunk. He began unloading several pieces of luggage while the woman hovered, cautioning him not to handle anything too roughly. At last the man emerged from the taxi. He checked to make sure all the luggage was out of the trunk before counting out some money into the driver's waiting hand. They turned to speak to the doorman and Vicky said quickly to the driver, "I'm in a terrible hurry to get home."

"Okay, miss, hop in."

But before she could open the door, the portly man turned back. "Just a moment. I believe I left my newspaper in the taxi."

Nearly screaming with frustration, Vicky dived into the back and thrust a carefully folded newspaper into his hands. She slammed the door and leaned forward urgently.

"Can we get out of here now?"

A tall man in a short-sleeved blue shirt strode rapidly along Seaview Avenue. He turned in at number 19, unlatching the gate and walking quickly around the side of the house. He looked up at the kitchen window, which was open a few inches. Putting down the paper sack he was carrying, he pushed the window open wider.

Using the camellias to screen his movements, the man pulled out a can of lighter fluid. He uncorked it and squirted its contents over the bundle of rags in the paper sack. Then he pushed the sack through the open window. Holding onto it gingerly with one hand, he flicked his cigarette lighter with the other and lit the edge of the sack. As the flame took hold, he dropped the sack on the floor inside. He held the lighter to the kitchen window curtains until they too were burning.

The man stood outside the window until he was sure the fire had caught. A steady crackling noise came from the kitchen and he nodded in satisfaction. He shoved the can of lighter fluid into his pocket and walked briskly to the front of the house. Letting himself out through the gate, he moved down the sidewalk to the blue Chevy Nova parked at the curb. He got in and started the engine. As he passed number 19, he glanced at the smoke trickling out through the kitchen window. Then he turned left onto West Channel and accelerated toward the Pacific Coast Highway.

Matt's van rolled north on the Coast Highway. He turned on his right blinker as he neared the Chattauqua-West Channel intersection. As he rounded the corner, a blue Chevy Nova came toward him, passing a car in front and slipping over into Matt's lane. Matt wheeled toward the curb and swore under his breath. People who drove rental cars always seemed to act as if they owned the road.

He turned onto Seaview and wondered if Vicky and Ben were back yet. Her car wasn't in the drive... Matt slammed on the brakes. Smoke was pouring out of the back of the house, and flames leapt from the windows. Thank God they're out, he thought as he jumped out of his van. He unlatched the front gate and walked into the yard. Even here, the heat was incredible. The elderly man next door came out of his house and called to Matt, "I just called the fire department." He watched the flames licking up the exterior walls above the windows. "Terrible, ain't it? The boy's out okay, I suppose?"

"Boy? You mean Ben?" Just then, Matt heard the first high cry of a child, barely audible above the noise of the fire. "My God! Ben!" Matt shouted to the child and heard his answering cry. Grabbing his sport jacket out of the van, Matt ran with it to the outside garden faucet and soaked the jacket in water. He tented the sopping jacket over his head and shouldered open the front door. Smoke billowed out, engulfing him as he ran into the house.

"Ben? Ben! Where are you?" he called. Following the boy's cries, he stumbled through the house to Ben's room.

Ben was huddled in a corner of his bedroom, while the curtains and bed coverings crackled in flame. The room was filled with smoke, and Matt groped his way to Ben's side.

"Come on now, fella. I'm going to give you a ride out of here."

He wrapped the still-soggy sport jacket around Ben's shoulders and tucked it over his red hair. "Hang on, Ben." Scooping the child up in his arms, he lurched out of the room and through the smoke-filled house. Gasping and coughing, he stumbled out the front door in time to hear the scream of sirens approaching the house.

Behind the fire engines came a taxi. Vicky had been worried about her neighbors until she saw that it was her own house in flames.

"Stop!" she screamed at the cabbie and flung open the passenger door. Stumbling, falling, picking herself up, she ran toward her home. Tears streamed down her cheeks as she shoved her way through the crowd that had gathered on the sidewalk. "My son's in there! Someone *do* something!"

It wasn't until she was almost to her front yard that she saw them. Matt's hair was singed, and there were smudge marks on his forehead and cheeks. Ben's eyes were wide. Still wrapped in Matt's ruined jacket, but no longer crying, he was soberly watching the firemen playing their hoses on the flames.

Sobbing with relief, Vicky raced the last few yards and threw her arms around them.

Chapter 10

The last burly fireman stomped out of Vicky's house and said to her, "Better have someone board this place up, ma'am, until they come to fix it. Your phone's working. Call your insurance company and find yourself a motel room."

"How badly is it damaged?" Vicky asked fearfully. From the amount of activity and the length of time the firemen had been there, she assumed that the front wall was hiding nothing but a pile of rubble.

But the fireman said, "Not bad. Aside from smoke damage, not bad at all. Of course, your kitchen is totally gone, and the drapes and bedding in the back will have to be replaced, but all in all, it's lucky we got here when we did."

"Oh, thank you," she said quickly. "You all did a tremendous job."

"That's what we're here for, ma'am." He wiped his brow and then headed for the waiting fire truck.

Ben was standing on the sidewalk gazing up in awe. As the fireman swung on board, he called, "Goodbye, sonny," and off they went.

Vicky stood uncertainly on the front lawn, then she said to Matt, "Well, I guess I'd better call the insurance company. Thank goodness my desk is okay; I'd never find their number otherwise. Keep an eye on Ben, will you? I couldn't handle any more troubles." She turned hesitantly toward the front door, then took a deep breath and walked in.

The place was a shambles, and it made Vicky sick to look at it. She found her little phone book and began to dial.

When she came out a few minutes later, Matt and Ben were discussing the advisability of being a fireman. She told Matt that her insurance would pay for a motel for the time being. "And I'm registering under an assumed name," she announced with determination. "I can't believe this happened! What did that Whitney man say to you, anyway?"

Matt hadn't had a chance to tell her about his experience in Arizona, but he did so now. "I'm not quite sure how to go about locating him here. His secretary is smarter than I gave her credit for. I may have to wait until he gets back to Phoenix." Suddenly Matt gave Vicky a puzzled look. "Why did you come home in a taxi? Where's your car?"

"It wouldn't start and I had to leave it in the parking lot. That's another thing I'll have to take care of. I guess I'll just rent a car for now, and then—"

"A rental car! That's it!" Matt exclaimed.

"What?" Vicky's voice had a lifeless quality, as if there had been one emergency too many.

"When I was driving up West Channel, a guy in a rental car passed me going the other way. He was driving like a maniac, that's why I noticed him. I bet it was whoever set fire to the house—it may even have been Charles Whitney!"

"How did you know it was a rental car?" Vicky asked dazedly.

"It had one of those red-and-white decals on the rearview mirror—I can't remember if those are Hertz or Avis. But don't you see? If Charles Whitney rented a car, we can probably track him down." He jumped to his feet and went inside. Dialing the number for Avis, he composed his story.

"Hello, I'm hoping you can help me. I was with Mr. Charles Whitney this afternoon, and I left some very important papers in his car. I believe he rented the car from you. I desperately need the papers and I'm leaving for Portland soon. But I don't know where Mr. Whitney is staying in L.A."

"Just a moment." The voice at the other end was friendly. "Let me look it up." After a pause, she came back on the line. "I'm sorry, I don't seem to have any record of a car for a Mr. Charles Whitney."

"Well, I'm sure it was an Avis—it had one of those red stickers with white stripes on the rearview mirror."

"That's not ours, sir." Her voice was frosty now. "That's Hertz."

"Oh. Thanks." He hung up on her "Thank you for calling Avis," and looked up the number for Hertz.

The young-sounding woman at the airport Hertz office was also friendly and efficient, but she sounded doubtful. "We don't keep a record of where our customers are staying, sir. But let me just check."

Matt waited impatiently while she looked through the file. Finally she picked up the phone again. "Well, you're in luck," she said cheerfully. "Mr. Whitney had his car delivered to the airport Angeleno Inn on Monday, so I would guess that's where he's staying."

"Thanks very much," Matt said.

"Oh, it was no trouble. I hope you get those papers back."

"Yes, I'll be able to track him down now. Thanks again."

Matt hung up and stood staring at the phone and thinking. At last, with an evil smile, he picked up the phone again and dialed.

"Airport Angeleno Inn," said a nasal voice at the other end.

"Mr. Charles Whitney, please."

"One moment."

Click-click. Brr-brr. Brr-brr.

"Yes?"

Matt mentally crossed his fingers. "Can I speak to Joann?"

The man on the other end sounded slightly annoyed. "There's no one here by that name; they've connected you to the wrong room."

Quickly Matt said, "Isn't this 319?"

Sounding more irritated, the man replied, "No, this is 548."

"Oh damn, they gave me the wrong connection. Can you get the operator on the line?"

"No." The man spoke with finality. "Try calling back."

Matt replaced the receiver gently and walked

outside. Smiling triumphantly, he said to Vicky, "I found him."

Vicky had pulled herself together by this time. She looked up at Matt. "That's great. Let's go and see him and get this over with."

He shook his head. "You're not coming, it's too dangerous. I want to make sure nothing else is going to happen to you and Ben. But they won't do anything to me—they wouldn't take the chance."

"No, Matt. If it's that dangerous, we should call the police."

"And tell them what? No, Vicky, it's only dangerous for you and Ben, not for me. Gather up whatever you need and I'll drop you two off at the hotel. Then I'm going to see Charles Whitney."

At the Miramar Hotel in Santa Monica, Vicky went in to register while Matt and Ben waited in the van. When she came out, she was smiling.

"They're almost full up—all they had left was a two bedroom suite. Good thing the insurance company is paying for this!"

Matt chuckled. "Good. You go up and get settled. Why don't you give Ben his supper here? Then, when I get back, we'll get a sitter and go out to celebrate."

"Sounds wonderful." She handed him a matchbook. "I picked this up at the desk. Our room number is written inside."

Matt opened the matchbook. "Sixteen-ten. Okay."

Vicky gave him a "V" sign. "See you soon good luck."

She turned to walk into the hotel. Matt called her back. In a lowered voice he said, "Don't you think you'd better tell me what name you registered under?"

She grinned. "Ask for Margaret Sloan."

He smiled back at her. "Where did that come from?"

"It's mine, my middle and maiden names."

"Okay, Maggie, see you later."

Matt drove off, the cheerful grin he had given Vicky now replaced by a look of grim foreboding. Would Charles Whitney still be at his hotel, and more important, would he believe Vicky was sincere in her desire not to have the money? For the first time, Matt reflected that even as Ben was a walking time bomb for Charles Whitney and his plans, Charles Whitney was the same thing for Ben and Vicky. Would they ever really be safe?

He parked the van in the lot at the Angeleno Inn, and walked through the lobby to the elevators. A couple of blue-haired ladies were discussing their next day's bus tour of the stars' homes, and one businessman stood glumly in the rear. Matt knew his type; he'd be back down in the bar for the opening minutes of Happy Hour and find a perky young girl he could persuade to go with him to dinner at the Proud Bird. Then he'd bully a table by the window so that they could listen on the wall earphones to the pilots taking their pre-landing instructions from the tower. They would try to pick out which plane in the group approaching the runways was speaking. He'd pay for expensive steaks for both of them on his company credit card, and insist on cognac after dinner. Then he'd take her back to the hotel and suggest a nightcap in the bar. He'd do it all the right way, but he'd never score. Matt stole a look at him again. Too bad, his kind never did.

The ladies got off on the second floor, still tittering happily; Gregory Peck's new home in some area called Holmby Hills was their first stop.

The businessman got off on three, and Matt rode alone up to five. As the elevator doors opened, he stepped out and looked down in surprise at the clenched fists hanging at his sides. The thought suddenly flashed through his mind that he'd really like to beat the shit out of Charles Whitney. The man was a snake; he would be a threat to Vicky and Ben forever. Calm down, he told himself. The only way you can really help is by talking to this guy on his own level. He realized that it wouldn't get him anywhere to walk in with both fists flying. No, he had to keep calm, keep cool, and talk rationally.

Matt tapped at the door of room 548. The man who opened the door had dark sandy hair and shrewd green eyes. His receding hairline made him appear older than his years. But he was certainly Charles Whitney. Matt recognized immediately the same hawklike nose and air of almost haughty arrogance that he'd noticed in Tom the first time he saw him. Somehow Matt hadn't anticipated this forcible reminder of Tom. In all his thoughts about what Charles Whitney had done, or tried to do, Matt realized he had pushed aside the knowledge that this man was Tom's brother.

"Charles Whitney? I'm Matt London." Matt stuck out his hand for Charles Whitney to shake, and at the same time edged forward through the doorway. His college experience in selling encyclopedias came flooding back; in a moment he was standing in the motel room with the door closed behind him and Charles Whitney staring at him in distaste.

Another man got up from the couch. He was tall and had a beer-belly hanging over his belt, but underneath the flab, Matt sensed a layer of hard muscle.

"Now that you're in, what do you want?" Charles asked disagreeably.

"I want you to leave Ben Hunter alone," Matt said evenly.

Charles turned his back to Matt in dismissal and walked toward the window. "I don't know who you're talking about. Maybe you'd better get out of here."

Matt ignored his seeming lack of interest. "Ben Hunter," he went on calmly. "Vicky and Tom Hunter's child. You remember Tom. You knew him as Lloyd Thomas Whitney, your older brother."

Charles Whitney turned, one eyebrow raised. "My brother? Do you know something about Lloyd?"

"I know that he changed his name to Tom Hunter." Matt pulled a folded paper from his pocket and extended it to Whitney. "Here's a copy of the court order."

Charles took the paper and read through it rapidly. "This is very interesting. As you may know, we've been looking for Lloyd. How can I get in touch with him?"

Matt laughed shortly. "I think you know that won't be possible. Lloyd is dead."

"Dead!" Charles's surprise sounded almost genuine.

"Yes. Now his son is all that stands between you and the entire Whitney fortune."

Charles paced across the room, staring through the expanse of glass at the traffic below. Then he faced Matt again with an apologetic smile. "You'll understand that this comes as something of a shock, Mr.— London, was it? I'll certainly let my lawyers know so we can follow up this lead. I'm very grateful that you brought this information to me." He glanced at the other man. "Hand me my checkbook, Ralph." Smiling again at Matt, he went on, "I'd like to express my appreciation. How much do you think—"

Matt broke in angrily, "Don't think you can buy me off. You know perfectly well that Ben is your brother's son. That's why you've been trying to kill him."

Charles looked at him expressionlessly. "I have no idea what you're talking about. Perhaps you'd better explain."

"Stop playing games, Whitney. Vicky told me about the man who lured Ben into the street and the car that ran her off the road. And I was around for that business at the pool and the hit-and-run attempt. You almost got lucky then, but that old lady is pretty tough and you missed the kid entirely. You've been pretty sloppy, or maybe you just hire incompetents." Ralph opened his mouth, but Charles silenced him with a glance. Matt went on, "However, drugging the boy and leaving him to die in the mountains was pushing things, and arson was the last straw. It's got to stop." He paused, but before he could continue, Charles spoke.

"That's quite a bizarre tale. Tell me, has this child, whoever he is, actually been harmed?"

"You know he hasn't, but—"

"I see." Charles nodded. "You and your young lady friend have worked out a clever little scheme. Or perhaps you planned it all by yourself? Unfortunately, people in my position have to learn to deal with phonies who crawl out from under the rocks from time to time. Did you ever actually meet my brother, or did you just hear about him on the news?"

"We were roommates for two years in college," Matt said steadily.

Charles smiled tightly. "So you've made a career out of trying to latch onto the Whitney money. It must have been hard to wait around until my father died. Or did you put the bite on Lloyd first? What actually happened to my brother?"

Matt's eyebrows drew together in a puzzled frown. What was Whitney getting at? At last he said slowly, "Not that I believe this is news to you, but Lloyd was electrocuted in a motel room shower in Arizona. The police called it an accident, but I don't think it was. Lloyd had a phobia about using things like radios in a bathroom."

The silence hung ominously. Charles Whitney took four deliberate steps toward the window. He turned, his features a grim mask. Green eyes narrowed, he held Matt's gaze in a calculating stare. His manicured nails clicked as he tapped them slowly on the top of the console television. Finally he spoke in measured tones. "I think you're right. It doesn't sound like an accident. And you seem to know a lot about it. Where were you the night Lloyd died?"

Matt's mind reeled.

—Whitney's going to try to pin Lloyd's murder on me!

His horror grew as he realized how plausible it could be made to sound. Whitney's money could buy any amount of manufactured evidence and testimony; he probably had several judges in his financial pocket. And Matt's own involvement with Vicky and Ben could easily be twisted to look suspiciously ugly. He was the perfect fall guy.

Matt felt defeated; Whitney seemed to hold all the cards. He thought despairingly of Vicky. He hadn't managed to help her at all; in fact, he'd made things worse.

Matt watched Whitney's impassive face. The guy

would be hell at a poker table. Then a thought flashed through Matt's mind. Maybe two could play at that game.

He turned to Ralph. "Too bad you did such a clumsy job setting that fire, Ralph. It didn't get near the garage. That's where all Lloyd's stuff was stored—including the radio the cops sent back with his effects."

Matt forced a slow grin across his stiff features. "It was hot that night in Arizona. I bet you didn't bother to wear gloves. I wonder what the police will think when they match up your prints with the ones on the radio and the plug."

Ralph looked uncertainly at Charles Whitney and his face grew red. "Christ, C.W.—"

"Shut up, Ralph."

Ralph ignored Whitney's warning tone. "But C.W., you said everything was taken care of—"

"I said shut up."

Matt shook his head slowly. "You know, Ralph, I think old C.W. played you for a sucker."

Ralph wheeled to face him. "That's all you know, smartass. C.W. backs me up every time. He always has things planned out."

Still shaking his head, Matt replied, "Yeah, but I don't think he planned this particular get-together. And you've got a big mouth, Ralph."

Turning back to his employer, Ralph said, "C.W.?..."

His voice trailed off. A small but efficient-looking revolver had appeared in Whitney's hand.

"C.W.?"

Standing very still, Matt said quietly, "Now wait a minute, Whitney..."

Ignoring Matt, Charles said, "I'm sorry, Ralph, but

the man's right. You do have a big mouth."

In one smooth movement, Charles Whitney raised the gun and fired. From a distance of two feet, the bullet tore into the soft tissue of Ralph's lower jaw. Ripping upward through the base of his brain, it lodged in the back of his skull. His eyes still wide in astonishment, Ralph sat down heavily. He was dead before his head hit the floor.

The revolver's muzzle was now aimed unwaveringly at Matt. He stood motionless, but his mind was racing furiously.

"Well, Mr. London, it certainly is unfortunate that you came to my hotel room while I was out and only Ralph was here. You must have threatened him, and Ralph pulled this gun."

He paused. Matt watched him in silence.

"I'm going to be terribly shocked when I return and find that the two of you have killed each other. But before I do, I have an errand to take care of. Where are Mrs. Hunter and the boy?"

"I don't know."

"Come, come, Mr. London, you can do better than that."

Matt said evenly, "I said I don't know."

"Very well. Empty your pockets one at a time, and put everything on the dresser beside you."

Without moving, Matt eyed the distance between them. Whitney was too far away—Matt could never reach him before he pulled the trigger. But if Whitney would just come a little closer...

"I'm becoming impatient, Mr. London. Don't make me hurt you more than I have to."

Matt reached slowly into his right-hand pocket and drew out a handful of change. Soon there was a small heap of coins on the dresser top, along with his handkerchief and wallet.

"Toss the wallet to me," Whitney instructed him, "slowly and carefully."

Keeping the gun pointed steadily at Matt, he quickly sorted through the wallet. The small amount of currency and Matt's driver's license and Visa card held no interest for him. Whitney sighed dramatically. "You're making this very difficult, Mr. London. Turn out your pockets."

Reluctantly, Matt obeyed. The matchbook from the Miramar fluttered to the floor.

"That's more like it, Mr. London. I can see you're not a smoker. Just toss that matchbook over here as well."

Matt bent to pick it up, and then straightened. Hesitating for just an instant, he sailed the matchbook across the room toward the man with the gun. Whitney's eyes left Matt momentarily as he reached out to catch it. In that instant, Matt's other hand shot out. Scooping up the loose change on the dresser top, he hurled the coins at Whitney's face.

Three shots came in rapid succession. Matt was flung to the floor, one arm trapped beneath him. Pain seared through his left side, and he felt the warm stickiness of blood.

Charles Whitney glanced down at Matt's still form and the dark red stain seeping into the carpet beneath his head. Then he flipped the matchbook open and read the penciled number—1610.

Dropping the revolver into his jacket pocket, Whitney walked quickly to the door. He opened it and glanced up and down the corridor. Satisfied, he strode briskly toward the elevator.

In the parking lot, Charles Whitney slid behind the wheel of his Thunderbird. He gunned it out of the lot onto Sepulveda and moved left for the Lincoln Boulevard turnoff. The speedometer edged up to sixty as he barreled along the wide divided roadway, his eyes on the alert for traffic patrols.

The room seemed to be fading in and out of focus. Matt shook his head to clear his muzzy brain, and then winced as the edges of a broken rib grated on one another. He tried to sit up, and gasped. Pain shot through him, and the blood began to ooze again from the wound in his side.

He couldn't see very well. He brushed his sleeve across his eyes and it came away covered with blood.

Gritting his teeth, Matt pulled himself up and leaned heavily against the dresser. He lurched to the bathroom and supported himself on the sink, breathing hard. Blood plopped steadily on the tile floor. He stared into the mirror. He'd been damned lucky. One bullet had messed up a couple of ribs, but it didn't seem to have hit much else. Most of the blood was coming from the side of his head. The second bullet must have creased his scalp as he fell. He thought he remembered a third shot. God knew where it had gone, but he had more important things to worry about.

Grabbing a towel, he turned on the cold water and soaked it, then wiped the blood from his face and head. He dropped the reddened towel in the sink and pulled a dry one from the rack. Fighting off nausea, he tied it clumsily around his ribcage. That should hold it for a while. As he wadded the two skimpy hand towels into a compress for his head, he thought: I have to warn Vicky.

Matt staggered into the room. The phone seemed miles away.

—How long was I out? Christ, I have no idea.

He nearly tripped over Ralph's inert body, and half-fell on the nearest bed. Was it already too late? He struggled to reach the phone and dialed the hotel operator.

"Get me the Miramar Hotel."

"I'm sorry, sir, you have to dial your local calls. Just hang up and dial nine, and then the number."

"But I don't have the number."

"Just one moment, sir, I'll ring Information. When you get the number, be sure to dial nine first."

"But—" His protest was cut off and he listened in frustration to the ringing tone. At last he heard, "Information. For what city?"

"Santa Monica, the Miramar Hotel." His pulse pounded as he waited in impotent fury.

"I have your number," she informed him at last. "Please make a note of it for future use. For the Miramar Hotel, the number is 510-8787."

Savagely, he punched the disconnect button. Adrenalin coursing through his system made his hand shake as he stabbed at the dial.

"Miramar Hotel," came the answer a moment later.

"Room 1610."

When Vicky answered, he said hoarsely, "Thank God."

"Matt?" She sounded alarmed.

"Yes. Listen, Vicky, there's no time to explain. Charles Whitney is on his way to the Miramar, and he's got a gun. Lock all your doors and call the cops. Stay right where you are and don't open the door for anyone."

"Matt! Are you all right?"

"Just do as I say. I'll be in touch."

Disconnecting again, he dialed zero.

"May I help you?"

"Get me the police." Even in his anxiety, he grinned wryly at the sound of that classic line.

"I'm sorry, sir, you have to dial your local calls. Just dial nine—"

He broke in, "Listen, there's a dead man here in my room. Will you just get the goddam police on the phone?"

There was a shocked intake of breath from the other end of the line. Then Matt heard her putting through the call.

Through the pain that threatened to engulf him, Matt struggled to gather his thoughts.

—I've got to sound rational and coherent—there's no time to waste.

When the desk sergeant answered, Matt said, "Please listen carefully. My name is Matthew London. I am in room 548 of the Airport Angeleno Inn. I have been shot and wounded, and another man has been shot and killed, by a man named Charles Whitney. Whitney is on his way now, with a gun, to kill Mrs. Vicky Hunter and her son Ben. They are in the Miramar Hotel in room 1610."

He paused for breath. "Charles Whitney is about six feet tall, with green eyes and sandy hair. He's armed and dangerous. Please get there as fast as you can. That's room 1610 at the Miramar."

He dropped the receiver and fell back exhausted on the bed.

Vicky tied Ben's other sneaker and stood up. Grabbing

her purse, she said tensely, "Come on, sweetie, we have to go right now."

"But, Mom—"

She grasped his hand tightly and walked him briskly to the door of the suite. Opening the door, she took a cautious look down the hall. It was completely deserted. She pulled Ben out of the room and closed the door behind them. Her face was the color of putty and her voice was brittle, but she strove to sound reassuring.

"We're going down to see the man who runs this hotel, honey, and then we're going to get in a taxi and go and see Jimmy. Won't that be fun?"

"Where's Matt, Mom?"

Her voice breaking, she said, "We'll see him later."

Vicky pushed the "down" button and watched the numbers light up as the elevator slowly ascended. A sigh of relief escaped her as the doors slid open.

A man stepped out. His green eyes bored into hers. "Mrs. Hunter?"

The doors slid closed behind him. "And this must be Ben."

She stared in fascinated horror as he slowly drew the gun from his pocket.

"I think we'll be more comfortable in your room—1610, isn't it?"

He gestured with the gun. Dumbly, Vicky turned. She clutched Ben's hand close to her as Charles Whitney herded them back down the hall.

The elevator doors opened on the sixteenth floor. The three uniformed policemen leaning against the wall straightened up as the watch commander stepped into the hall. Four other men followed him out of the elevator. Three were in uniform; the fourth was Matt London. His face pale and his eyes glassy, he was running on pure adrenalin at this point.

Sergeant Wu came up to report. "All units are in place, sir. We're just waiting for the hostage negotiator, Dr. Lindquist, to arrive.

"What's the situation now?" the commander asked.

"We have ascertained that Charles Whitney is inside the room—suite 1610. The hostages are a woman and her young son. They are unharmed so far. Whitney has told us, and the woman has confirmed, that he is holding a gun on the child. He says if we make any attempt to break in, he'll shoot." Lowering his voice, he added, "He sounds pretty ragged, sir."

The commander nodded heavily. "What's your setup?"

"We've evacuated this entire floor and those immediately above and below. Of course, we've got men on the doors and sharpshooters on the balconies, but we can't get a direct line into the room. They've all got strict orders to hold tight."

"Good." The commander looked down the hall. "What kind of gun is he using?"

The uniformed lieutenant who had ridden up with him in the elevator spoke up. "Assuming it's the one he used at the Airport Angeleno, it's a .22-caliber handgun. If he's reloaded, he's probably got six shots."

"A Saturday-night special." The commander sounded disgusted.

"Yes, sir, but at close range it can do a lot of damage."

He could kill them both! A wave of despair washed over Matt. Through the roaring in his ears, he heard the commander say, "Well, nothing to do now but wait. It's the old defensive lineup."

His words triggered something in Matt. Suddenly his eyes focused. A few yards away, at the end of the hall, was the door to 1610. Behind it, Vicky and Ben waited in the clutches of a madman.

The roaring in his ears grew louder. Over it he seemed to hear, *You've got the ball, boy. Run with it.*

Head down and elbows out, Matt plunged forward. Taking them by surprise, he burst through the knot of officers clustered by the elevator doors. He ran, dodging and weaving. A blue-uniformed body materialized in front of him. Matt threw out his hip and sidestepped neatly. Where the hell was his blocker?

He heard the crowd screaming. He was going to make it! But here came two more of the opposing team's defense. Matt ran straight into one of them, knocking him down, and spun around out of reach of the second man. Only ten yards to go.

The roaring merged with the pounding in his head as he stumbled the last few steps. There it was. Matt hurled himself between the two officers guarding the door. "Vicky! Vick-y!"

Inside the room, Vicky's heart seemed to stop. "Matt! Get back! He's got a gun!"

Whitney's precarious control snapped. Slinging Ben aside, he jumped to his feet.

"I killed you! You're already dead!" he screamed. He leveled his revolver at the door. The bullets thudded into the wood. Vicky grabbed Ben and yanked him behind the couch. Whitney kept squeezing the trigger. Now there was only a series of clicks.

Outside, the two husky officers pulled Matt to his

feet. One of them smashed his rifle butt into the door. Two quick shoves, and they were inside.

Whitney was still firing the empty gun point-blank at the door. When he saw the policemen coming toward him, he threw his gun at them and ran back to the terrace.

"Stop! Stop or I'll shoot!" called one of the cops.

Whitney paid no attention. His cool and haughty demeanor was totally gone now. He scurried like a rat across the balcony.

The sharpshooter on the neighboring terrace pointed his rifle. "Hold up, buster. We've got you covered."

Whitney climbed over the railing and prepared to drop to the balcony below.

"Stop! This is the police."

The single warning shot rang out.

Charles Whitney let go of the railing. His scream lasted for the entire sixteen-floor drop.

Chapter 11

By the next evening, Vicky and Ben's suite had been restored to order. Acting with unusual speed, the hotel management had brought in overtime help to change the door and install newer and larger color televisions in both bedrooms. Two dozen yellow roses graced the coffee table in the living room, along with a huge basket of fresh fruit. Rumor traveled fast, and the management was not unaware of the size of the Whitney fortune.

Matt pushed his straight-backed chair away from the table and stood up stiffly. He was uncomfortably aware of the tight bandages strapping his ribcage. Leaning against the mantelpiece, he smiled wearily.

"Nice dinner."

Vicky glanced from him to Ben. "Yes. It's good to have a peaceful, relaxed evening for a change."

Looking at Ben's half-empty plate, she added, "Finished, honey?"

"Yeah."

"Was your hamburger good?"

"Yeah, it was neat," he said with enthusiasm. "And I like those skinny french fries. Can I have them again tomorrow?"

Vicky laughed. "Sure, why not?"

"I like it here." Ben climbed down from his chair.

Noticing the bluish shadows under his eyes, Vicky said, "Good. But now I think it's time for you to jump into bed. Say goodnight to Matt."

When he was tucked in, Vicky came back to the living room of the suite. Both she and Matt had spent the entire day dealing with a succession of lawyers, police officials, doctors, and the media. Now that they were alone together, an air of constraint seemed to pervade the atmosphere.

At last, Matt broke the awkward silence. Raising his wineglass, he said, "Here's to the newest Whitney heir."

He took a sip of wine as Vicky stared at him without expression. Looking around the well-appointed room, Matt added, "He seems to be taking to the life of luxury easily enough."

"No, Matt, that's not the way it's going to be."

She refilled her own wineglass as Matt raised an inquiring eyebrow. "Oh?"

"I think I've gotten things straightened out with the lawyers. Of course, there's all kinds of legal mumbo-jumbo to sort out, but they know what I want. I've decided to liquidate the Whitney Company entirely. All the money will be put in a trust fund for Ben. That seems to be the best solution."

"I see." Matt watched her, his gaze revealing nothing.

Vicky rushed on, "I don't know anything about running a big company, and I have no desire to learn. Of course, there will still be a lot of decisions I'll have to make as I deal with the trust fund. But at least I won't be perpetuating the Whitney Company and its methods. They've caused enough grief. I want to wipe that name out forever."

"Well," Matt said after a moment, "sounds like you'll have the power to do whatever you want. You're becoming quite the lady executive."

Vicky's cheeks flushed a little at his tone. She turned to stare out the window.

"You know, Matt," she said more slowly, "it seems there was a lot about Tom that I didn't know; I'm just beginning to learn that. But the part of Tom I didn't know was the Whitney part. I want to keep it that way. The Tom Hunter I married is the Tom I want to remember. Can you understand that?"

"Oh, I understand. You've got everything neatly sorted out and compartmentalized. Of course, it will be Whitney money that supports you while you build a shrine to Tom Hunter's memory. You'll be able to go on living in the past forever."

Vicky whirled to face him. "I can't believe you're saying these things. You were Tom's friend." She glared at him angrily, the spots of color deepening on her cheeks.

Before he could answer, they heard Ben's wail of terror. His cries mounted as Vicky raced into his bedroom, Matt right behind her.

Ben was huddled against the wall in the corner of the

bed. Vicky bent and picked him up. "Ben, honey, you're okay." But his tense body squirmed and twisted in her arms. He opened his eyes and saw Matt standing beside the bed. Wrenching himself out of Vicky's grasp, he threw himself at Matt and locked his little arms convulsively around Matt's neck.

Matt stroked Ben's back gently. "It's okay now. It's all over." He looked at Vicky. "It's the fire. That's how I found him, all scrunched up in a corner."

He continued murmuring softly to Ben as the boy's fear subsided. His sobs diminished to shuddering breaths. Still keeping a firm hold on Matt, he said shakily, "Mommy?"

"I'm here, sweetheart." She touched his face.

"Matt?"

"I'm here, Ben. It's all okay now."

Matt sat down on the bed. In a few moments, he eased Ben down, still stroking him reassuringly. Vicky watched as her son's eyelids began to droop. She tiptoed quietly out.

In the living room, Vicky looked around uncertainly. Wandering across to the fireplace, she paused to stare at herself in the mirror and run her fingers quickly through her hair.

—Poor Matt. He's gone through so much, and it was all to help me and Ben. I've been so selfish, so wrapped up in my own problems, I've hardly even thanked him for saving our lives.

Matt closed the bedroom door quietly behind him. "He's asleep. I guess it's about time for me to take off."

"Wait," she said. He turned expectantly.

"I feel terrible, Matt. You must think I'm really ungrateful. You've done so much, risking your life and almost getting killed, and in all the commotion, I've never really thanked you. How can I ever repay you?"

He gave her a twisted smile. "That's okay. Next time you're in trouble, just give me a call."

Vicky stared at him. She'd said it all wrong—it had come out sounding like Lady Bountiful. But she couldn't think how to say what she felt.

Matt waited for a moment. When she didn't speak, he said quietly, "Good luck, Vicky. I hope everything turns out well for you." He raised his hand in a gesture of farewell, and then walked toward the door.

Vicky watched as he unlocked the door and reached for the doorknob. In a moment he'd be out of her life forever.

"Don't leave." She wasn't sure whether she'd thought those words or spoken them aloud. Matt hesitated, his hand on the doorknob.

Her voice was low, but she spoke steadily. "I'm not still in love with Tom. It was over long ago, but it's taken me until just now to realize it."

He turned slowly. And then she was across the room, her arms around him, her lips on his.

"Oh, Matt," she breathed at last.

He kissed her with tender urgency, and Vicky responded wholeheartedly. She knew that, from now on, nothing would stand between them.

★ ★ ★ ★ ★ ★
JOHN JAKES'

KENT FAMILY CHRONICLES

Stirring tales of epic adventure and soaring romance which tell the story of the proud, passionate men and women who built our nation.

☐	05686-3	THE BASTARD (#1)	$2.75
☐	05238-8	THE REBELS (#2)	$2.50
☐	05371-6	THE SEEKERS (#3)	$2.50
☐	05684-7	THE FURIES (#4)	$2.75
☐	05685-5	THE TITANS (#5)	$2.75
☐	04047-9	THE WARRIORS (#6)	$2.25
☐	04125-4	THE LAWLESS (#7)	$2.25
☐	05432-1	THE AMERICANS (#8)	$2.95

Available at your local bookstore or return this form to:

JOVE BOOK MAILING SERVICE
1050 Wall Street West
Lyndhurst, N.J. 07071

Please send me the titles indicated above. I am enclosing $_____ (price indicated plus 50¢ for postage and handling for the first book and 25¢ for each additional book). Send check or money order—no cash or C.O.D.'s please.

NAME_____

ADDRESS_____

CITY_____STATE/ZIP_____

Allow three weeks for delivery. SK-17